Little Sarah lay in the space between her daddy's chest and arm, snuggled against him in a pose of trust. Danny looked naturally capable. Grace wished she had a camera.

Careful not to disturb Danny, she reached down and lifted Sarah from his arms. The baby sniffled and stretched, but Grace "shhhhed" her back to sleep and laid her in her crib.

"Danny?"

He grumbled something unintelligible, and she smiled. Damn, he was cute. It really didn't seem fair that she had to resist him.

"Danny, if you don't want to get up, I can sleep in your room. But you'll have to wake up with Sarah when she cries for her two-o'clock feeding."

The threat of being responsible for Sarah must have penetrated, because he took a long breath, then groggily sat up. He stared at her, as if needing to focus, and reached for her hand, which was still on his shoulder. His fingers were warm and his touch gentle, sending reaction from Grace's fingertips to her toes.

In the silence of the dark night their gazes stayed locked for what felt like forever.

Dear Reader,

This has been quite a year for me! It was exciting to be asked to write for Harlequin Romance®, and to have an opportunity to create stories with emotional depth that are sure to tug at your heartstrings.

Grace and Danny are two very special characters, and their story will always be one of my favorites. It's never easy when a twist of fate changes the course of two people's lives. But when there's a baby involved, everything takes on even greater meaning. Grace and Danny rise to the occasion, providing us with a touching love story that will stay with us for a long time.

By the way, Sarah is named after my own daughter, and I used a lot of her mannerisms and personality traits to create Grace and Danny's little girl. My Sarah's not a baby anymore, but some things a mother never forgets! Like the way she loves her dad. Even as a baby, Sarah could wrap my big strong husband around her little finger!

I hope you enjoy this book and the future Harlequin Romance novels that are in the planning stages!

Susan

SUSAN MEIER

Her Pregnancy Surprise

TORONTO • NEW YORK • LONDON
AMSTERDAM • PARIS • SYDNEY • HAMBURG
STOCKHOLM • ATHENS • TOKYO • MILAN • MADRID
PRAGUE • WARSAW • BUDAPEST • AUCKLAND

ISBN-13: 978-0-373-03981-4
ISBN-10:   0-373-03981-6

HER PREGNANCY SURPRISE

First North American Publication 2007.

Copyright © 2007 by Linda Susan Meier.

Printed in U.S.A.

Susan Meier spent most of her twenties thinking she was a job-hopper—until she began to write, and realized everything that came before was only research! One of eleven children, with twenty-four nieces and nephews and three kids of her own, Susan has had plenty of real-life experience watching romance blossom in unexpected ways. She lives in western Pennsylvania with her wonderful husband, Mike, her three children and her two overfed, well-cuddled cats, Sophie and Fluffy. You can visit Susan's Web site at www.susanmeier.com.

Susan says: "The beautiful beach house my family rented for vacation last summer was the inspiration for Danny's Virginia Beach house. I took a few liberties with the decorating—I've always wanted red leather sofas—but the ocean view and the wonderful deck are very real, making that house the perfect getaway for Danny and Grace!"

I'd like to thank my editors, Katinka Proudfoot
and Suzy Harding, and also
Senior Editor Kim Young, for helping me
turn Grace and Danny's story into a real keeper.

CHAPTER ONE

"YOU AREN'T planning on driving back to Pittsburgh tonight, are you?"

Danny Carson walked into the third floor office of his Virginia Beach beach house talking to Grace McCartney, his newest employee, who stood behind his desk, hunched over her laptop. A tall brunette with bright violet eyes and a smile that lit the room, Grace was smart, but more than that she was likable and she genuinely liked people. Both of those qualities had helped enormously with the work they'd had to do that weekend.

Grace looked up. "Would you like me to stay?"

"Call it a debriefing."

She tilted her head to one side, considering the suggestion, then smiled. "Okay."

This was her real charm. She'd been working every waking minute for three days, forced to spend her entire weekend assisting Danny as he persuaded Orlando Riggs—a poor kid who parlayed a basketball scholarship into a thirty-million-dollar NBA deal—to use Carson Services as his financial management firm. Not only was she away from her home in Pittsburgh and her friends, but she hadn't gotten to relax on her days off. She could be annoyed that he'd asked her to stay another night. Instead she smiled. Nothing ruffled her feathers.

"Why don't you go to your room to freshen up? I'll tell Mrs. Higgins we'll have dinner in about an hour."

"Sounds great."

After Grace left the office, Danny called his house-keeper on the intercom. He checked his e-mail, checked on dinner, walked on the beach and ended up on the deck with a glass of Scotch. Grace took so long that by the time Danny heard the sound of the sliding glass door opening behind him, Mrs. Higgins had already left their salads on the umbrella table and their entrées on the serving cart, and gone for the day. Exhausted from the long weekend of work, and belatedly realizing Grace probably was, too, Danny nearly suggested they forget about dinner and talk in the morning, until he turned and saw Grace.

Wearing a pretty pink sundress that showed off the tan she'd acquired walking on the beach with Orlando, she looked young, fresh-faced and wholesome. He'd already noticed she was pretty, of course. A man would have to be blind not to notice how attractive she was. But this evening, with the rays of the setting sun glistening on her shoulder-length sable-colored hair and the breeze off the ocean lightly ruffling her full skirt, she looked amazing.

Unable to stop himself he said, "Wow."

She smiled sheepishly. "Thanks. I felt a little like celebrating Orlando signing with Carson Services, and though this isn't exactly Prada, it's the best of what I brought."

Danny walked to her place at the table and pulled out her chair. "It's perfect." He thought about his khaki trousers, simple short-sleeved shirt and windblown black hair as he seated her, then wondered why he had. This wasn't a date. She was an employee. He'd asked her to stay so he could give her a bonus for the good job she'd done that week, and to talk to her long enough to ascertain the position into which he should promote her—also to thank her for doing a good job. What he wore should be of no consequence. The fact that it even entered his head nearly made him laugh.

He seated himself. "Mrs. Higgins has already served dinner."

"I see." She frowned, looking at the silver covers on the plates on the serving cart beside the table, then the salads that sat in front of them. "I'm sorry. I didn't realize I had stayed in the tub so long." She smiled sheepishly again. "I was a little more tired than I thought."

"Then I'm glad you took the extra time." Even as the words tumbled out of his mouth, Danny couldn't believe he was saying them. Yes, he was grateful to her for being so generous and kind with Orlando, making the athlete feel comfortable, but the way Danny had excused her lateness sounded personal, when he hardly knew this woman.

She laughed lightly. "I really liked Orlando. I think

he's a wonderful person. But we were still here to do a job. Both of us had to be on our toes 24/7."

When she smiled and Danny's nerve endings crackled to life, he realized he was behaving out of character for a boss because he was attracted to her. He almost shook his head. He was so slow on the uptake that he'd needed an entire weekend to recognize that.

But he didn't shake his head. He didn't react at all. He was her boss and he'd already slipped twice. His "wow" when he'd seen her in the dress was inappropriate. His comment about the extra time that she'd taken had been too personal. He excused himself for those because he was tired. But now that he saw what was happening, he could stop it. He didn't date employees, but also this particular employee had proven herself too valuable to risk losing.

Grace picked up her salad fork. "I'm starved and this looks great."

"Mrs. Higgins is a gem. I'm lucky to have her."

"She told me that she enjoys working for you because you're not here every day. She likes working part-time, even if it is usually weekends."

"That's my good fortune," Danny agreed, then the conversation died as they ate their salads. Oddly something inside of Danny missed the more personal chitchat. It was unusual for him to want to get friendly with an employee, but more than that, this dinner had to stay professional because he had things to discuss with her. Yet he couldn't stop the surge of disappointment, as if he were missing an unexpected opportunity.

When they finished their salads, he rose to serve the main course. "I hope you like fettuccini alfredo."

"I love it."

"Great." He removed the silver covers. Pushing past the exhaustion that had caused him to wish he could give in and speak openly with her, he served their dinners and immediately got down to business. "Grace, you did an exceptional job this weekend."

"Thanks. I appreciate the compliment."

"I intend to do more than compliment you. Your work secured an enormous account for Carson Services. Not only are you getting a bonus, but I would like to promote you."

She gaped at him. "Are you kidding?"

Pleased with her happy surprise, Danny laughed. "No. Right now you and I need to talk a bit about what you can do and where in the organization you would like to serve. Once we're clear, I'll write up the necessary paperwork."

She continued to stare at him slightly openmouthed, then she said, "You're going to promote me anywhere I want to go?"

"There is a condition. If a situation like Orlando's ever comes up again, where we have to do more than our general push to get a client to sign, I want you in on the persuading."

She frowned. "I'm happy to spend time helping a reluctant investor see the benefits of using your firm, but you don't need to promote me for that."

"The promotion is part of my thank-you for your assistance with Orlando."

She shook her head. "I don't want it."

Positive he'd heard wrong, Danny chuckled. "What?"

"I've been with your company two weeks. Yet I was the one chosen for a weekend at your beach house with Orlando Riggs—a superstar client most of the men and half of the women on staff were dying to meet. You've already given me a perk beyond what employees who have been with you for years have gotten. If there's an empty position somewhere in the firm, promote Bobby Zapf. He has a wife and three kids and they're saving for a house. He could use the money, and the boost in confidence from you."

Danny studied her for a second, then he laughed. "I get it. You're joking."

"I'm serious." She took a deep breath. "Look, everybody understood that you chose me to come with you this weekend because I'm new. I hadn't worked with you long enough to adopt your opinions, so Orlando knew that when I agreed with just about everything you said I wasn't spouting the company party line. I hadn't yet heard the party line. So I was a good choice for this. But I don't want to be promoted over everybody's head."

"You're worried about jealousy?"

She shook her head. "No! I don't want to take a job that should go to someone else. Someone who's worked for you for years."

"Like Bobby Zapf."

"In the two weeks I spent at the office, I watched

Bobby work harder than anybody else you employ. If you want to promote somebody he's the one."

Danny leaned back in his chair. "Okay. Bobby it is." He paused, toyed with his silverware, then glanced up at her, holding back a smile. He'd never had an employee turn down a promotion—especially not to make sure another person got it. Grace was certainly unique.

"Can I at least give you a bonus?"

She laughed. "Yes! I worked hard for an entire weekend. A bonus is absolutely in order."

Continuing to hold back a chuckle, Danny cleared his throat. "Okay. Bonus, but no promotion."

"You could promise to watch my performance over the next year and then promote me because I'd had enough time to prove myself."

"I could." He took a bite of his dinner, more pleased with her than anybody he'd ever met. She was right. In his gratitude for a weekend's work, he had jumped the gun on the promotion. She reeled him in and reminded him of the person who really deserved it. If he hadn't already been convinced she was a special person, her actions just now would have shown him.

Grace smiled. "Okay. It's settled. I get a bonus and you'll watch how well I work." Then as quickly as she'd recapped their agreement, she changed the subject. "It's beautiful here."

Danny glanced around. Darkness had descended. A million stars twinkled overhead. The moon shone like a silver dollar. Water hit the shore in white-foamed waves.

"I like it. I get a lot of work done here because it's so quiet. But at the end of the day I can also relax."

"You don't relax much, do you?"

Lulled by the sounds of the waves and her calming personality, Danny said, "No. I have the fate of a company that's been around for decades on my shoulders. If I fail the company fails and the legacy my great-grandfather sweated to create crumbles into nothing. So I'm focused on work. Unless relaxation happens naturally, it doesn't happen."

"I don't relax much, either." She picked up her fork again. "You already heard me tell Orlando I grew up the same way he did. Dirt poor. And in the same away he used his talent to make a place for himself, I intend to make a place for myself, too."

"Here's a tip. Maybe you shouldn't talk your bosses out of promotions?"

"I can't take what I don't deserve." She wiggled her eyebrows comically. "I'll just have to make my millions the old-fashioned way. I'll have to earn them."

Danny laughed and said, "I hate to tell you this, but people who work for someone else rarely get rich. So if you want to make millions, what are you doing working for me?"

"Learning about investing. When I was young I heard the theory that your money should work as hard for you as you work for it. Growing up, I didn't get any experience seeing how to make money work, so I figured the best place to get the scoop on investing was at an investment firm." She smiled, then asked, "What about you?"

"What about me?"

She shrugged. "I don't know. Anything. Did you want your family's business? Were you a happy child? Are you happy now?" She shrugged again. "Anything."

She asked the questions then took a bite of her dinner, making her inquiry into his life seem casual, offhand. But she'd nonetheless taken the conversation away from herself and to him. Still, she didn't seem as if she were prying. She seemed genuinely curious, but not like a bloodhound, like someone trying to become a friend.

He licked his suddenly dry lips and his heart rate accelerated as he actually considered answering her. A part of him really wanted to talk. A part of him *needed* to talk. Two years had passed. So much had happened.

He took a breath, amazed that he contemplated confiding in her, yet knowing he wouldn't. Though he couldn't ignore her, he wouldn't confide. He'd never confide. Not to her. Not to anyone.

He had to take the conversation back where it belonged. To business.

"What you see is who I am. Chairman of the Board and CEO of Carson Services. There isn't anything to talk about."

She blinked. "Really?"

"From the time I was six or eight I knew I would take over the company my great-grandfather started. I didn't have to travel or experiment to figure out what I wanted. My life was pretty much mapped out for me and I simply followed the steps. That's why there's not a lot to talk about."

"You started training as a kid?"

"Not really training, more or less being included in on conversations my dad and grandfather thought were relevant."

"What if you didn't like investing?"

"But I did."

"It just sounds weird." She flushed. "Sorry. Really. It's none of my business."

"Don't be sorry." Her honesty made him laugh. More comfortable than he could remember being in years, he picked up his fork and said, "I see what you're saying. I was lucky that I loved investing. I walked into the job as if it were made for me, but when my son—"

He stopped. His chest tightened. His heart rate kicked into overdrive. He couldn't believe that had slipped out.

"But your son what?"

"But when my son began to show artistic talent," he said, thinking quickly because once again the conversation had inadvertently turned too personal. And this time it was *his* fault. "I suddenly saw that another person might not want to be CEO of our company, might not have the ability to handle the responsibility, or might have gifts and talents that steer him or her in a different direction. Then the company would have to hire someone, and hiring someone of the caliber we would require would involve paying out a huge salary and profit sharing. The family fortune would ultimately deplete."

She studied him for a second, her gaze so intense Danny knew the mention of his son had her curious. But he wouldn't say any more about Cory. That part of his life was so far off-limits that he didn't even let himself think about it. It would be such a cold, frosty day in hell that he'd discuss Cory with another person that he knew that day would never come.

Finally Grace sighed. "I guess you were lucky then—" she turned her attention back to her food "—that you wanted the job."

Danny relaxed. Once again she'd read him perfectly. She'd seen that though he'd mentioned his son, he hadn't gone into detail about Cory, and instead had brought the discussion back to Carson Services, so she knew to let the topic go.

They finished their dinner in companionable conversation because Grace began talking about remodeling the small house she'd bought when she got her first job two years before. As they spoke about choosing hardwood and deciding on countertops, Danny acknowledged to himself that she was probably the most sensitive person he'd met. She could read a mood or a situation so well that he didn't have to worry about what he said in front of her. A person who so easily knew not to pry would never break a confidence.

For that reason alone an intense urge to confide in her bubbled up in him, shocking him. Why the hell would he want to talk about the past? And why would he think that any woman would want to hear her boss's marital horror stories? No woman would. No *person* would. Except maybe a gossip. And Grace wasn't a gossip.

After dinner, they went inside for a drink, but Danny paused beside the stairway that led to his third-floor office suite.

"Bonuses don't pass through our normal accounting. I write those checks myself. It's a way to keep them completely between me and the employees who get them. The checkbook's upstairs. Why don't we just go up now and give you your bonus?"

Grace grinned. "Sounds good to me."

Danny motioned for Grace to precede him up the steps. Too late, he realized that was a mistake. Her perfect bottom was directly in his line of vision. He paused, letting her get a few steps ahead of him, only to discover that from this angle he had a view of her shapely calves.

He finished the walk up the stairs with his head down, gaze firmly fixed on the Oriental carpet runner on the steps. When he reached the third floor, she was waiting for him. Moonlight came in through the three tall windows in the back wall of the semidark loft that led to his office, surrounding her with pale light, causing her to look like an angel.

Mesmerized, Danny stared at her. He knew she was a nice person. A *good* person. He also knew that was why he had the quick mental picture of her as an angel and such a strong sense of companionship for her. But she was an employee. He was her boss. He needed to keep his distance.

He motioned toward his office suite and again she preceded him. Inside, he sat behind the desk and she gingerly sat on the chair in front of it.

"I think Orlando Riggs is the salt of the earth," Danny said as he pulled out the checkbook he held for the business. "You made him feel very comfortable."

"I felt very comfortable with him." She grimaced. "A lot of guys who had just signed a thirty-million-dollar deal with an NBA team would be a little cocky."

"A little cocky?" Danny said with a laugh. "I've met people with a lot less talent than Orlando has and a lot less cash who were total jerks."

"Orlando seems unaffected."

"Except that he wants to make sure his family has everything they need." Danny began writing out the check. "I didn't even realize he was married."

"And has two kids."

Kids.

Danny blinked at the unexpected avalanche of memory just the word kids brought. He remembered how eager he'd been to marry Lydia and have a family. He remembered his naive idea of marital bliss, and his chest swelled from the horrible empty feeling he got every time he realized how close he'd been to fulfilling that dream and how easily it had all been snatched away.

But tonight, with beautiful, sweet-tempered, sincere Grace sitting across the desk, Danny had a surprising moment of clarity. He'd always blamed himself for the breakdown of his marriage, but what if it had been Lydia's fault? He'd wanted to go to counseling. Lydia had simply wanted to *go*. Away from him. If he looked at the breakdown of his marriage from that very thin perspective, then the divorce wasn't his fault.

That almost made him laugh. If he genuinely believed the divorce wasn't his fault then—

Then he'd wasted years?

No. He'd wasted his life. He didn't merely feel empty the way he'd been told most people felt when they lost a mate; he felt wholly empty. Almost nonexistent. As if he didn't have a life. As if every day since his marriage had imploded two years ago, he hadn't really lived. He hadn't even really existed. He'd simply expended time.

Finished writing the check, Danny rose from his seat. It seemed odd to think about feeling empty when across the desk, eager, happy Grace radiated life and energy.

"Thank you for your help this weekend."

As he walked toward her, Grace also rose. He handed her the check. She glanced down at the amount he'd written, then looked up at him. Her beautiful violet eyes filled with shock. Her tongue came out to moisten her lips before she said, "This is too much."

Caught in the gaze of her hypnotic eyes, seeing the genuine appreciation, Danny could have sworn he felt some of her energy arch to him. If nothing else, he experienced a strong sense of connection. A rightness. Or maybe a purpose. As if there was a reason she was here.

The feeling of connection and intimacy could be nothing more than the result of spending every waking minute from Friday afternoon to Sunday night together, but that didn't lessen its intensity. It was so strong that his voice softened when he said, "No. It isn't too much. You deserve it."

She took a breath that caused her chest to rise and fall, calling his attention to the cleavage peeking out of the pink lace of her dress. She looked soft and feminine, yet she was also smart and sensitive. Which was why she attracted him, tempted him, when in the past two years no other woman had penetrated the pain that had held him hostage. Grace treated him like a person. Not like her rich boss. Not like a good catch. Not even like a guy so far out of her social standing that she should be nervous to spend so much one-on-one time. But just like a man.

"Thanks." She raised her gaze to his again. This time when Danny experienced the sense of intimacy, he almost couldn't argue himself out of it because he finally understood it. *She* felt it, too. He could see it in her eyes. And he didn't want to walk away from it. He *needed* her.

But then he saw the check in her hands and he remembered she was an employee. An affair between them had consequences. Especially when it ended. Office gossip would make him look foolish, but it could ruin her. Undoubtedly it would cost her her job. He might be willing to take a risk because his future wasn't at stake, but he couldn't make the decision for her.

CHAPTER TWO

DANNY cleared his throat. "You're welcome. I very much appreciated your help this weekend." He stepped away and walked toward the office door. "I'm going downstairs to have a drink before I turn in. I'll see you in the morning."

Grace watched Danny go, completely confused by what was happening between them. For a few seconds, she could have sworn he was going to kiss her and the whole heck of it was she would have let him.

Let him? She was so attracted to him she darned near kissed him first, and that puzzled her. She should have reminded herself that he was her boss and so wealthy they were barely on the same planet. Forget about being in the same social circle. But thoughts of their different worlds hadn't even entered her head, and, thinking about them now, Grace couldn't muster a reason they mattered.

Laughing softly, she combed her fingers through her hair. Whatever the reason, she couldn't deny the spark between her and Danny. When Orlando left that afternoon, Grace had been disappointed that their weekend together had come to an end. But Danny had asked her to stay one more night, and she couldn't resist the urge to dress up and hope that he would notice her the way she'd been noticing him. He'd nearly ruined everything by offering her a promotion she didn't deserve, but he showed her that he trusted her opinion by taking her advice about Bobby Zapf.

The real turning point came when he mentioned his son. He hadn't wanted to talk about him, but once Danny slipped him into the conversation he hadn't pretended he hadn't. She had seen the sadness in his eyes and knew there was a story there. But she also recognized that this wasn't the time to ask questions. She'd heard the rumor that Danny had gone through an ugly divorce but no report had mentioned a child from his failed marriage. Nasty divorces frequently resulted in child custody battles and his ex-wife could very well make him fight to see his son, which was undoubtedly why he didn't want to talk about him.

But tonight wasn't the night for probing into a past that probably only reminded him of unhappy times. Tonight, she had to figure out if he felt for her what she was beginning to feel for him. The last thing she wanted was to be one of those employees who got a crush on her boss and then pined for him for the rest of her career.

And she wouldn't get any answers standing in his third floor office when he was downstairs!

She ran down the steps and found him in the great room, behind the bar, pouring Scotch into a glass.

He glanced up when she walked over. Though he seemed surprised she hadn't gone to her room as he'd more or less ordered her to, he said, "Drink?"

Wanting to be sharp and alert so she didn't misinterpret anything he said or did, Grace smiled and said, "No. Thanks."

She slid onto one of the three red leather bar stools that matched the red leather sofas that sat parallel to each other in front of the wall of windows that provided a magnificent view of the Atlantic Ocean. A black, red and tan Oriental rug between the sofas protected the sand-colored hardwood floors. White-bowled lights connected to thin chrome poles suspended from the vaulted ceiling, illuminating the huge room.

Danny took a swallow of his Scotch, then set the glass on the bar. "Can't sleep?"

She shrugged. "Still too keyed up from the weekend I guess."

"What would you normally do on a Sunday night?"

She thought for a second, then laughed. "Probably play rummy with my mother. She's a cardaholic. Loves any game. But she's especially wicked with rummy."

"Can't beat her?"

"Every once in a while I get lucky. But when it comes to pure skill the woman is evilly blessed."

Danny laughed. "My mother likes cards, too."

Grace's eyes lit. "Really? How good is she?"

"Exceptional."

"We should get them together."

Danny took a long breath, then said, "We should."

And Grace suddenly saw it. The thing that had tickled her brain all weekend but had never really surfaced. In spite of her impoverished roots and his obviously privileged upbringing, she and Danny had a lot in common. Not childhood memories, but adult things like goals and commitments. He ran his family's business. She was determined to help her parents out of poverty because she loved them. Even the way they viewed Orlando proved they had approximately the same beliefs about life and people.

If Danny hadn't asked for her help this weekend, eventually they would have been alone together long enough to see that they clicked. They matched. She knew he realized it, too, if only because he'd nearly slipped into personal conversation with her four times at dinner, but he had stopped himself. Probably because she was an employee.

It was both of their loss if they weren't mature enough to handle an office relationship. But she thought they were. Her difficult childhood and his difficult divorce had strengthened each of them. They weren't flip. They were cautious. Smart. If any two people could have an office relationship without it affecting their work, she and Danny were the two. And she wasn't going to miss out on something good because, as her boss, Danny wouldn't be the first to make a move.

She raised her eyes until she caught his gaze. "You know what? Though you're trying to fight it, I think you like me. Would it help if I told you I really like you, too?"

* * *

For several seconds, Danny didn't answer. He couldn't. He'd never met a woman so honest, so he wasn't surprised that she spoke her mind. Even better, she hadn't played coy and tried to pretend she didn't see what was going on. She saw it, and she wanted to like him as much as he wanted to like her.

And that was the key. The final answer. She wanted to like him as much as he wanted to like her and he suddenly couldn't understand why he was fighting it.

"It helps enormously." He bent across the bar and kissed her, partly to make sure they were on the same page with their intentions, and partly to see if their chemistry was as strong as the emotions that seemed to ricochet between them.

It was. Just the slight brush of their lips knocked him for a loop. He felt the explosion the whole way to his toes.

She didn't protest the kiss, so he took the few steps that brought him from behind the bar and in front of the stool on which she sat. He put his hands on her shoulders and kissed her deeply this time, his mouth opening over hers.

White-hot desire slammed through him and his control began slipping. He wanted to touch her, to taste her, to feel all the things he'd denied himself for the past two years.

But it was one thing to kiss her. It was quite another to make love. But when he shifted away, Grace slid her hand around his neck and brought his lips back to hers.

Relief swamped him. He'd never had this kind of an all-consuming desire to make love. Yet, the yearning he felt wasn't for sexual gratification. It was to be with Grace herself. She was sweet and fun and wonderful…and beautiful. Having her slide her arms around him and return his kisses with a passion equal to his own filled him with an emotion so strong and complete he dared not even try to name it.

Instead he broke the kiss, lifted her into his arms and took her to his bed.

The next morning when Grace awoke, she inhaled a long breath as she stretched. When her hand connected with warm, naked skin, her eyes popped open and she remembered she'd spent the night making love with her boss.

Reliving every detail, she blinked twice, waiting for a sense of embarrassment or maybe guilt. When none came she smiled. She couldn't believe it, but it was true. She'd fallen in love with Danny Carson in about forty-eight hours.

She should feel foolish for tumbling in over her head so fast. She could even worry that he'd seen her feelings for him and taken advantage of her purely for sexual gratification. But she wasn't anything but happy. Nobody had ever made love to her the way he had. And she was sure their feelings were equal.

She yawned and stretched, then went downstairs to the room she'd used on Friday and Saturday nights. After brushing her teeth and combing her hair, she ran back to Danny's room and found he was still sleeping, so she slid into bed again.

Her movements caused Danny to stir. As Grace

thanked her lucky stars that she had a chance to fix up a bit before he awoke, he turned on his pillow. Ready, she smiled and caught his gaze but the eyes that met hers were not the warm brown eyes of the man who had made love to her the night before. They were the dark, almost black eyes of her boss.

She remembered again the way he'd made love to her and told herself to stop being a worrying loser. Yes, the guy who ran Carson Services could sometimes be a real grouch, but the guy who lived in this beach house was much nicer. And she was absolutely positive that was the real Danny.

Holding his gaze, she whispered, "Good morning."

He stared at her. After a few seconds, he closed his eyes. "Tell me we didn't make a mistake."

"We did not make a mistake."

He opened his eyes. "Always an optimist."

She scooted closer so she could rest her head on his outstretched arm. "We like each other. A lot. Something pretty special happened between us."

He was silent for a few seconds then he said, "Okay."

She twisted so she could look at him. "Okay? I thought we were fantastic!"

His face transformed. The caution slipped from his dark eyes and was replaced by amusement. "You make me laugh."

"It's a dirty job but somebody's got to do it."

Chuckling, he caught her around the waist and reversed their positions. But gazing into her eyes, he softened his expression again and said, "Thanks," before he lowered his head and kissed her.

They made love and then Danny rolled out of bed, suggesting they take a shower. Gloriously naked, he walked to the adjoining bathroom and began to run the water. Not quite as comfortable as he, Grace needed a minute to skew her courage to join him, and in the end wrapped a bedsheet around herself to walk to the bathroom.

But though she faltered before dropping the sheet, when she stepped into the shower, she suddenly felt bold. Knowing his trust was shaky because of his awful divorce, she stretched to her tiptoes and kissed him. He let her take the lead and she began a slow exploration of his body until he seemed unable to handle her simple ministrations anymore and he turned the tables.

They made love quickly, covered with soap and sometimes even pausing to laugh, and Grace knew from that moment on, she was his. She would never feel about any man the way she felt about Danny.

CHAPTER THREE

WHEN Grace and Danny stood in the circular driveway of his beach house, both about to get into their cars to drive back to Pittsburgh, she could read the displeasure in his face as he told her about the "client hopping" he had scheduled for the next week. He wanted to be with her but these meetings had been on the books for months and he couldn't get out of them. So she kissed him and told him she would be waiting when he returned.

They got into their vehicles and headed home. He was a faster driver, so she lost him on I-64, but she didn't care. Her heart was light and she had the kind of butterflies in her tummy that made a woman want to sing for joy. Though time would tell, she genuinely believed she'd found Mr. Right. She'd only known Danny for two weeks, and hadn't actually spent a lot of that time with him since he was so far above her on the company organizational chart. But the weekend had told her everything she needed to know about the real Danny Carson.

To the world, he was an ambitious, demanding, highly successful man. In private, he was a loving, caring, normal man, who liked her. A lot.

Yes, they would probably experience some problems because he owned the company she worked for. He'd hesitated at the bar before kissing her. He'd asked her that morning if they'd made a mistake. But she forced herself not to worry about it. She had no doubt that once they spent enough time together, and he saw the way she lived her beliefs, his worries about dating an employee would vanish.

What they had was worth a few months of getting to know each other. Or maybe the answer would be to quit her job?

The first two days of his trip sped by. He called Wednesday morning, and the mere sound of his voice made her breathless. Though he talked about clients, meetings, business dinners and never-ending handshaking, his deep voice reminded her of his whispered endearments during their night together and that conjured the memory of how he tasted, the firmness of his skin, the pleasure of being held in his arms. Before he disconnected the call, he whispered that he missed her and couldn't wait to see her and she'd all but fainted with happiness.

The next day he didn't call, but Grace knew he was busy. He also didn't call on Friday or Saturday.

Flying back to Pittsburgh Sunday, Danny nervously paced his Gulfstream, fighting a case of doubt and second thoughts about what had happened between him

and Grace. In the week that had passed, he hadn't had
a spare minute to think about her, and hadn't spoken
with her except for one quick phone call a few days into
the trip. The call had ended too soon and left him
longing to see her, but after three days of having no
contact, the negatives of the situation came crowding
in on him, and there were plenty of them.

First, he didn't really know her. Second, even if she
were the perfect woman, they'd gone too far too fast.
Third, they worked together. If they dated it would be
all over the office. When they broke up, he would be the
object of the same gossip that had nearly ruined his
reputation when his marriage ended.

He took a breath and blew it out on a puff. He
couldn't tell if distance was giving him perspective or
calling up all his demons. But he did know that he
should have thought this through before making love to
her.

Worse, he couldn't properly analyze their situation
because he couldn't recall specifics. All he remembered
from their Sunday night and Monday morning together
were emotions so intense that he'd found the courage
to simply be himself. But with the emotions gone, he
couldn't summon a solid memory of the substance of
what had happened between them. He couldn't remember anything specific she'd said to make him like her—
like? Did he say like? He didn't just like Grace. That
Sunday night his feelings had run more along the lines
of a breathless longing, uncontrollable desire, and total
bewitching. A man in that condition could easily be

seduced into seeing traits in a woman that weren't there and that meant he had made a horrible mistake.

He told himself not to think that way. But the logical side of his brain called him a sap. He'd met Grace two weeks before when she'd come to work for his company, but he didn't really know her because he didn't work with new employees. He worked with their bosses. He said hello to new employees in the hall. But otherwise, he ignored them. So he hadn't "known" her for two weeks. He'd glimpsed her.

Plus, she'd been on her best behavior for Orlando. She had been at the beach house to demonstrate to Orlando that Carson Services employed people in the know. Yes, she'd gone above and beyond the call of duty in her time with Orlando, making him feel comfortable, sharing personal insights—but, really, wasn't that her job?

Danny took a long breath. Had he fallen in love with a well polished persona she'd pulled out to impress Orlando and simply never disengaged when the basketball star left?

Oh Lord!

He sat, rubbed his hands down his face and held back a groan. Bits and pieces of their Sunday night dinner conversation flitted through his brain. She'd grown up poor. Could only afford a house that needed remodeling. She wanted to be rich. She'd gone into investing to understand money.

He *had* money.

Technically he was a shortcut to all her goals.

He swallowed hard. It wasn't fair to judge her when she wasn't there to defend herself.

He had to see her. Then he would know. After five minutes of conversation she would either relieve all his fears or prove that he'd gone too fast, told her too much and set himself up for a huge disappointment.

The second his plane taxied to a stop, he pulled out his cell phone and called her, but she didn't answer. He left a message but she didn't return his call and Danny's apprehensions hitched a notch. Not that he thought she should be home, waiting for him, but she knew when he got in. He'd told her he would call. He'd said it at the end of a very emotional phone conversation in which he'd told her that crazy as it sounded, he missed her. She'd breathlessly told him she missed him, too.

Now she wasn't home?

If he hadn't given her the time he would be landing, if he hadn't told her he would be calling, if he hadn't been so sappy about saying how much he missed her, it wouldn't seem so strange that she wasn't home. But, having told her all those things, he had the uncontrollable suspicion that something was wrong.

Unless she'd come to the same conclusions he had. Starting a relationship had been a mistake.

That had to be it.

Relief swamped him. He didn't want another relationship. Ever. And Grace was too nice a girl to have the kind of fling that ended when their sexual feelings for each other fizzled and they both eagerly walked away.

It was better for it to end now.

Content that not only had Grace nicely disengaged their relationship, but also that he probably wouldn't run into her in the halls because their positions in the company and the building were so far apart, he went to work happy. But his secretary buzzed him around ten-thirty, telling him Grace was in the outer office, asking if he had time for her.

Sure. Why not? Now that he'd settled everything in his head, he could handle a debriefing. They'd probably both laugh about the mistake.

He tossed his pencil to the stack of papers in front of him. "Send her in."

He steeled himself, knowing that even though his brain had easily resolved their situation, his body might not so easily agree. Seeing her would undoubtedly evoke lots of physical response, if only because she was beautiful. He remembered that part very, very well.

His office door opened and she stepped inside. Danny almost groaned at his loss. She was every bit as stunning as he remembered. Her dark hair framed her face and complemented her skin tone. Her little pink suit showed off her great legs. But he wasn't meant for relationships and she wasn't meant for affairs. Getting out now while they could get out without too much difficulty was the right thing to do.

"Good morning, Grace."

She smiled. "Good morning."

He pointed at the chair in front of his desk, indicating she should sit. "Look, I know what you're going to say. Being away for a week gave me some perspective, too, and I agree we made a mistake the night we slept together."

"What?"

Confused, he cocked his head. "I thought you were here to tell me we'd made a mistake."

Holding the arms of the captain's chair in front of his desk, she finally sat. "I came in to invite you to dinner."

He sat back on his chair, knowing this could potentially be one of the worst conversations of his life. "I'm sorry. When you weren't home last night when I called, I just assumed you'd changed your mind."

"I was at my mother's."

"I called your cell phone."

She took a breath. "And by the time I realized I'd hadn't turned it on after I took it off the charger, it was too late for me to call you back." She took another breath and smiled hopefully. "That's why I came to your office."

He picked up his pencil again. Nervously tapped it on the desk. "I'm sorry. Really. But—" This time he took the breath, giving himself a chance to organize his thoughts. "I genuinely believe we shouldn't have slept together, and I really don't want to see you anymore. I don't have relationships with employees."

He caught her gaze. "I'm sorry."

That seemed to catch her off guard. She blinked several times, but her face didn't crumble as he expected it would if she were about to cry. To his great relief, her chin lifted. "That's fine."

Pleased that she seemed to be taking this well—

probably because his point was a valid one—bosses and employees shouldn't date—he rose. "Do you want the day off or something?"

She swallowed and wouldn't meet his gaze. She said, "I'm fine," then turned and walked out of his office.

Danny fell to his seat, feeling like a class-A heel. He had hurt her and she was going to cry.

Grace managed to get through the day with only one crying spurt in the bathroom right after coming out of Danny's office. She didn't see him the next day or the next or at all for the next two weeks. Just when she had accepted that her world hadn't been destroyed because he didn't want her or because she'd slept with him, she realized something awful. Her female cycle was as regular as clockwork, so when things didn't happen on the day they were supposed to happen, she knew something was wrong.

Though she and Danny had used condoms, they weren't perfect. She bought an early pregnancy test and discovered her intuition had been correct. She had gotten pregnant.

She sat on the bed in the master suite of her little house. The room was awash with warm colors: cognac, paprika, butter-yellow in satin pillows, lush drapes and a smooth silk bedspread. But she didn't feel any warmth as she stared at the results of the EPT. She had just gotten pregnant by a man who had told her he wanted nothing to do with her.

She swallowed hard and began to pace the honey-yellow hardwood floors of the bedroom she'd scrimped, saved and labored to refinish. Technically she had a great job and a good enough income that she could raise a child alone. Money wasn't her problem. And neither was becoming a mother. She was twenty-four, ready to be a mom. Excited actually.

Except Danny didn't want her. She might survive telling him, but she still worked for him. Soon everybody at his company would know she was pregnant. Anybody with a memory could do the math and realize when she'd gotten pregnant and speculate the baby might be Danny's since they'd spent a weekend together.

He couldn't run away from this and neither could she.

She took a deep breath, then another, and another, to calm herself.

Everything would be fine if she didn't panic and handled this properly. She didn't have to tell Danny right away that she was pregnant. She could wait until enough time had passed that he would see she wasn't trying to force anything from him. Plus, until her pregnancy was showing, she didn't have to tell anybody but Danny. In six or seven months the people she worked with wouldn't necessarily connect her pregnancy with the weekend she and Danny together. They could get out of this with a minimum of fuss.

That made so much sense that Grace easily fell asleep that night, but the next morning she woke up dizzy, still exhausted and with an unholy urge to vomit. On Saturday morning, she did vomit. Sunday morning, she couldn't get out of bed. Tired, nauseated and dizzy beyond belief, she couldn't hide her symptoms from anybody. Which meant that by Monday afternoon, everybody would guess something was up, and she had no choice but to tell Danny first thing in the morning that she was pregnant. If she didn't, he would find out by way of a rumor, and she couldn't let that happen.

Grace arrived at work an hour early on Monday. Danny was already in his office but his secretary had not yet arrived. As soon as he was settled, she knocked on the frame of his open door.

He looked up. "Grace?"

"Do you have a minute?"

"Not really, I have a meeting—"

"This won't take long." She drank a huge gulp of air and pushed forward because there was no point in dilly-dallying. "I'm pregnant."

For thirty seconds, Danny sat motionless. Grace felt every breath she drew as the tension in the room increased with each second that passed.

Finally he very quietly said, "Get out."

"We need to talk about this."

"Talk about this? Oh, no! I won't give credence to your scheme by even gracing you with ten minutes to try to convince me you're pregnant!"

"Scheme?"

"Don't play innocent with me. Telling the man who

broke up with you that you're pregnant is the oldest trick in the book. If you think I'm falling for it, you're insane."

Grace hadn't expected this would be an easy conversation, but for some reason or another she had expected it to be fair. The Danny she remembered from the beach house might have been shocked, but he would have at least given her a chance to talk.

"I'm not insane. I am pregnant."

"I told you to get out."

"This isn't going to go away because you don't believe me."

"Grace, I said leave."

His voice was hard and cold and his office fell deadly silent. Knowing there was no talking to him in that state and hoping that after she gave him a few hours for her announcement to sink in he might be more amenable to discussing it, Grace did as he asked. She left his office with her head high, controlling the tears that welled behind her eyelids.

The insult of his reaction tightened her chest and she marched straight to her desk. She yanked open the side drawer, withdrew her purse and walked out of the building as if it were the most natural thing in the world for her to do. When she got into her car, she dropped her head to her steering wheel and let the tears fall.

Eventually it would be obvious she hadn't lied. But having Danny call her a schemer was the absolute worst experience she'd ever had.

Partially because he believed it. He believed she would trick him.

Grace's cheeks heated from a sudden rush of indignation.

It was as if he didn't know her at all—or she didn't know him at all.

Or maybe they didn't know each other.

She started her car and headed home. She needed the day to recover from that scene, but also as sick as she was she couldn't go back to work until she and Danny had talked this out. Pretty soon everybody would guess what had happened. If nothing else, they had to do damage control. There were lots of decisions that had to be made. So when she got home she would call her supervisor, explain she'd gotten sick and that she might be out a few days. Then she and Danny would resolve this *away* from the office.

Because she had written down his home number and cell number when he left the message on her answering machine the Sunday night he'd returned from his business trip, Grace called both his house and his cell that night.

He didn't answer.

She gave him forty-eight hours and called Thursday morning before he would leave for work. Again, no answer.

A little more nervous now, she gave him another forty-eight hours and called Saturday morning. No answer.

She called Monday night. No answer.

And she got the message. He wasn't going to pick up her calls.

But by that time she had something a little more serious to handle. She couldn't get well. Amazed that she'd even been able to go to work the Monday of her encounter with Danny, she spent her days in bed, until, desperate for help and advice, she told her mother that she was pregnant and sicker than she believed was normal. They made a quick gynecologist appointment and her doctor told her that she was simply enduring extreme morning sickness.

Too worried about her baby to risk the stress of dealing with Danny, Grace put off calling him. Her life settled into a simple routine of forcing herself out of bed, at least to the couch in her living room, but that was as far as she got, and watching TV all day, as her mother fussed over her.

Knowing the bonus she'd received for her weekend with Orlando would support her through her pregnancy if she were frugal, she quit her job. Swearing her immediate supervisor to secrecy in their final phone conversation, she confided that she was pregnant and having troubles, though she didn't name the baby's father. And she slid out of Carson Services as if she'd never been there.

She nearly called Danny in March, right before the baby was born, but, again, didn't have the strength to handle the complexities of their situation. Even though he would be forced to believe she hadn't lied, he might still see her as a cheat. Someone who had tricked him. She didn't know how to explain that she hadn't, and after nine months of "morning sickness" she didn't give a damn. A man who behaved the way he had wasn't her perfect partner. His money didn't make him the special prize he seemed to believe he was. It was smarter to focus on the joy of becoming a mother, the joy of having a child, than to think about a guy so hurt by his divorce that he couldn't believe anything anyone told him.

When Sarah was born everything suddenly changed. No longer sick and now responsible for a child, Grace focused on finding a job. Happily she found one that paid nearly double what she'd been making at Carson Services. Because her parents had moved into her house to help while she was pregnant, she surprised them by buying the little bungalow down the street. Her mother wanted to baby-sit while Grace worked. Her dad could keep up both lawns. And the mortgage on the new house for her parents was small.

Busy and happy, Grace didn't really think about Danny and before she knew it, it was September and Sarah was six months old. Everything from baby-sitting to pediatrician appointments was taken care of. Everyone in her little family was very happy.

And Grace wondered why she would want to tell Danny at all.

But holding Sarah that night she realized that this situation wasn't about her and Danny anymore. It was about Sarah. Every little girl had a right to know her daddy.

The following Saturday evening, Grace found herself craning her neck, straining to read the small sophisti-

cated street signs in the development that contained
Danny's house. It hadn't been hard to find his address.
Convincing herself to get in the car and drive over had
been harder. Ultimately she'd come to terms with it not
for Danny's sake, but for Sarah's. If Grace didn't at least
give Danny the chance to be a dad, then she was no
better than he was.

She located his street, turned onto it and immediately
saw his house. Simple stone, accented by huge multi-
paned windows, his house boasted a three-car garage
and space. Not only was the structure itself huge, but
beyond the fence that Grace assumed protected a
swimming pool, beautiful green grass seemed to stretch
forever before it met a wall of trees. Compared to her
tiny bungalow, his home was a palace.

She parked her little red car in his driveway, got out
and reached into the back seat to unbuckle Sarah.
Opting not to put her in a baby carrier, Grace pulled her
from the car and settled her on her arm.

Holding her squirming baby and bulky diaper bag,
she strode up the stone front walk to Danny's door,
once again noting the differences in their lifestyles per-
sonified by decorative black lantern light fixtures and
perfect landscaping.

Grace shook her head, trying to stop the obvious
conclusion from forming, but she couldn't. She and
Danny were different. Too difference to be together.
Why hadn't she recognized that? He probably had.
That's why he'd told her he didn't want to see her. They
weren't made for each other. Not even close. And he'd

now had fifteen months to forget her. She could have to explain the entire situation again, and then face another horrible scene.

Still, as much as she dreaded this meeting, and as much as she would prefer to raise Sarah on her own, she knew it wasn't fair for Sarah to never know her father. She also knew Danny should have the option to be part of his daughter's life. If he again chose not to believe Grace when she told him Sarah was his child, then so be it. She wouldn't beg him to be a father to their baby. She wouldn't demand DNA testing to force him in. If he wanted a DNA test, she would comply, but as far as she was concerned, she was the one doing him the favor. If he didn't wish to acknowledge his child or be a part of Sarah's life that was his decision. She wasn't going to get upset or let him hurt her again. If he said he wanted no part of her or her baby, this time Grace and Sarah would leave him alone for good.

Again without giving herself a chance to think, she rang the doorbell. Waiting for someone to answer, she glanced around at his massive home, then wished she hadn't. How could she have ever thought she belonged with someone who lived in this part of the city?

The door opened and suddenly she was face-to-face with the father of her child. Though it was Saturday he wore dress slacks and a white shirt, but his collar was unbuttoned and his tie loosened. He looked relaxed and comfortable and was even smiling.

Then his eyes darkened, his smile disappeared and

his gaze dropped to Sarah, and Grace realized he remembered who she was.

She took a breath. "Can we come in?"

The expression in his eyes changed, darkening even more, reminding Grace of a building storm cloud. For the twenty seconds that he remained stonily silent, she was positive he would turn her away. For those same twenty seconds, with his dark eyes condemning her, she fervently wished he would.

But without saying a word, he pulled open his door and stepped aside so she could enter.

"Thank you." She walked into the echoing foyer of his big house, fully expecting this to be the worst evening of her life.

CHAPTER FOUR

As GRACE brushed by Danny, a band of pain tightened his chest. At first he thought the contraction was a result of his anger with Grace, fury that she'd continued with her pregnancy scheme. He wondered how she intended to get around DNA since he would most certainly require the test, then he actually looked at the baby in her arms, a little girl if the pink one-piece pajamas were any indication. She appeared to be about six months old—the age their baby would be if he had gotten Grace pregnant that Sunday night at his beach house. More than that, though, the baby looked exactly as Cory had when he was six months old.

Danny stood frozen, unable to do anything but stare at the chubby child in Grace's arms. Suddenly the baby smiled at him. Her plump lips lifted. Her round blue eyes filled with laughter. She made a happy gurgling sound that caused playful spit bubbles to gather at the corners of her mouth. She looked so much like Cory it was as if Danny had been unceremoniously flung back in time.

Feeling faint, he pointed down the corridor. "There's a den at the end of the hall. Would you please wait for me there?"

Grace caught his gaze with her pretty violet eyes and everything inside of Danny stilled. In a hodgepodge of pictures and words, he remembered bits and pieces of both the weekend they'd spent together with Orlando and the morning he'd kicked her out of his office— wrongly if his assumptions about the baby were correct. In his mind's eye, he saw Grace laughing with Orlando, working with him, making him comfortable. He remembered her soft and giving in his arms. He remembered her trembling when she told him she was pregnant, and then he remembered nothing but anger. He hadn't given her a chance to explain or even a sliver of benefit of the doubt. He'd instantly assumed her "pregnancy" was a ruse and wouldn't hear another word.

"I don't think we want to be interrupted," he said, grasping for any excuse that would give him two minutes to come to terms with some of this before he had to talk to her. "So I need to instruct my house-keeper that we're to be left alone."

She pressed her lips together, nodded and headed down the hall. Once Danny saw her turn into the den, he collapsed on the bottom step of the spiral staircase in his foyer and dropped his head to his hands.

They were shaking. His knees felt like rubber. Pain ricocheted through him and he squeezed his eyes shut. In vivid detail, he saw Cory's birth, his first birthday party, and every Christmas they'd had together. He remembered his giggle. He remembered his endless questions as he grew from a toddler into a little boy. He remembered how he loved garbage trucks and mailmen.

Pain overwhelmed him as he relived every second of the best and worst six years of his life and then realized he could very well go through it all again. The first birthday. Laughing, happy Christmases. Questions and curiosities. And pain. One day he was a doting dad and the next he was living alone, without even the possibility of seeing his son again.

He fought the anger that automatically surged up in him when the thought about his marriage, about Lydia. In the past year, his sense of fair play had compelled him to examine his marriage honestly and he had to admit that Lydia hadn't been a horrible shrew. *He* hadn't been a terrible husband. Their marriage hadn't ended because he and his ex-wife were bad people, but because they'd hit a crossroad that neither had anticipated. A crossroad where there had been no choice but to separate. They had once been the love of each other's life, yet when their marriage had begun to crumble, they'd both forgotten the eight good years, only remembered their horrible final year, and fought bitterly. They'd hurt each other. Used Cory as a weapon. And both of them had walked away damaged.

Remembering that only made his upcoming showdown with Grace more formidable. He and Grace didn't have two years of courtship and six years of marriage to look back on to potentially keep them from hurting each other. So how did he expect their confrontation to turn out any better than his fight with Lydia had?

He didn't.

He wouldn't shirk his responsibility to Grace's baby. But he had learned enough from the past that the key to survival was not being so in love with his daughter that she could turn into Grace's secret weapon.

Finally feeling that he knew what he had to do, Danny rose from the step, went to the kitchen and told his housekeeper he and Grace weren't to be disturbed, then he walked to the den.

Unfortunately he couldn't keep the displeasure out of his voice when he said, "Let me see her."

Grace faced him. "Save your anger, Danny. I was the one left to have this baby alone. I was so sick I had to quit my job and depend on my parents to basically nurse me for nine months. The bonus you gave me went to support me until I had Sarah and could go back to work. I was sick, exhausted and worried that if anything went wrong when she was born I wouldn't be able to pay for proper care. You could have helped me through all of that, but you never even followed up on me. So the way I see this, you don't have anything to complain about."

She was right, of course. It didn't matter that he was still hurting from the end of his marriage when she told him she was pregnant. He hadn't for two seconds considered Grace or her feelings. Still, he had no proof that she was the innocent victim she wanted him to believe she was. The weekend they'd spent together, he'd made himself an easy mark for a woman he really didn't know. He'd never wanted another relationship, let alone a child. And now he had one with a stranger. A woman he genuinely believed had tricked him.

"What made it all worse was wondering about your reaction when I did bring Sarah to you." She sat on the leather sofa in the conversation area, laid the gurgling baby on the cushion and pulled the bonnet ribbon beneath the little girl's chin, untying the bow.

Danny's breathing stuttered as he stared at the baby. *His daughter.* A perfect little pink bundle of joy. She punched and pedaled her legs as Grace removed her bonnet.

Grace's voice softly intruded into his thoughts. "I understood when you told me you didn't want to see me anymore. I had every intention of respecting that, if only because of pride. But this baby was both of our doing."

Sarah spit out her pacifier and began to cry.

Grace lifted the little girl from the sofa cushion and smoothed her lips across her forehead. "I know. I know," she singsonged. "You're hungry."

She rose and handed the baby to Danny. "Can you take her while I get her bottle?"

Panic skittered through him and he backed away. He hadn't held a baby since Cory.

To his surprise Grace laughed. "Come on. She won't bite. She doesn't have teeth yet."

"I've…I'm…I just—"

Realizing he was behaving like an idiot, Danny stopped stuttering. He wasn't an idiot. And he would always think of Cory every time he looked at Sarah, but there was no way he'd admit that to Grace. She already knew enough about him and he didn't know half as much about her. Seeing Cory every time he looked at Sarah would be his cross to bear in private.

He reached out to take the baby, but this time Grace pulled her back.

"Sit," she said as if she'd thought his hesitancy was uncertainty about how to hold the baby. "I'll hand her to you."

Deciding not to argue her assumption, Danny lowered himself to the sofa and Grace placed the baby in his arms. "Just set her bottom on your lap, and support her back with your left hand."

He did that and the baby blinked up at him, her crying becoming sniffles as she lost herself to confusion about the stranger holding her.

Staring at her mutely, Danny identified. The first time he'd seen Cory was immediately after he'd slid into the doctor's hands. He'd been purple and wrinkled and when the doctor slapped his tiny behind he'd shrieked like a banshee. The little girl on Danny's lap was clean and now quiet. The total opposite of her half brother.

Grace pulled a bottle from her diaper bag. Dripping formula onto her wrist, she checked the bottle's temperature and said, "Can I take this to your kitchen and warm it?"

"Go back to the foyer, then turn right. The door at the end of the hall leads to the kitchen. My housekeeper is there. She'll help you."

Grace nodded and left.

Danny glanced down at the blue-eyed, rather bald baby. He took a breath. She blinked at him again, as if still confused.

"I'm your father."

She cocked her head to the right. The same way Cory used to. Especially when Danny would tell him anything about Carson Services, about responsibility, about carrying on the family name, as if the idea of doing anything other than paint was absurd.

Remembering Cory's reaction tightened Danny's chest again, but this time it wasn't from the memory of how, even as a small child, Cory had seemed to reject the idea of taking over the family business. Danny suddenly realized this little girl was now the one in line to run Carson Services. Grace might not know it, but Danny did.

Grace ran to the kitchen and didn't find a housekeeper, but she did locate a microwave into which she quickly shoved the bottle. She'd never seen a person more uncomfortable with a baby than Danny appeared to be, which was surprising considering he had a son, but she wasn't so insensitive that she didn't realize that meeting Sarah hadn't been easy for him.

She'd been preoccupied with Sarah's needs and hadn't factored Danny's shock into the equation. But having watched his facial expression shift and change, she realized that though he might not have believed Grace when she told him she was pregnant he seemed to be accepting that Sarah was his.

When the timer bell rang, she grabbed the bottle and

headed back to his den. Walking down the hall she heard Danny's soft voice.

"And that's why mutual funds are better for some people."

Grace stopped just outside the door.

"Of course, there are times when it's more logical to put the money of a conservative investor in bonds. Especially a nervous investor. Somebody who can't afford to take much risk. So you always have to question your investor enough that you can determine the level of risk his portfolio and personality can handle."

Standing by the wall beside the door, Grace twisted so she could remain hidden as she peered inside. Sarah gripped Danny's finger and stared up at him. Her blue eyes sharp and alert. Danny appeared comfortable, too, holding the baby loosely on his lap, and Grace realized that talking about something familiar was how Danny had overcome his apprehensions. Still, stocks? Poor Sarah!

"It's all about the individual. Some people are afraid of the stock market. Which is another reason mutual funds are so great. They spread the risk over a bunch of stocks. If one fails, another stock in the fund could sky-rocket and balance everything out."

If it had been under any other circumstances, Grace would have burst out laughing. Danny looked up and saw her standing there. He grimaced. "Sorry. I didn't know what else to talk about."

She shrugged. "I guess it doesn't really matter. All a baby really cares about is hearing your voice." She walked into the room and lifted Sarah from Danny's lap.

Nestling the baby into the crook of her arm, she added, "When in doubt, make up something. Maybe a story about a bunny or a bear. Just a short little anything."

Danny didn't reply, but rose and walked to the window. "You should be the one to sit."

Not about to remind him that there was plenty of space for both of them on the leather sofa, Grace took the place he had vacated. With two silent parents, the sound of Sarah greedily sucking filled the room.

"I almost wish you hadn't brought her to me."

Grace hadn't forgotten that he'd broken up with her before she told him she was pregnant. Still, that was his tough luck. He'd created a child and she wasn't letting him pretend he hadn't.

"She's your child."

"Yes. And I know you think there are all kinds of reasons that's great, but you're not going to like the way this has to play out."

"The way this has to play out?"

"I have to raise my daughter."

Not expecting that, Grace stared at his stiff back. But rather than be offended by his defiant stance, she remembered the feeling of his corded muscles beneath her fingertips. The firmness of his skin. Her own shivers of delight from having his hands on her.

Reaction flared inside her but she quickly shook it off. She wouldn't let herself fall victim to his charm again. Too much was at stake. She didn't know the official definition of "raise his daughter," but it sounded as if he intended to get more than a Saturday afternoon with Sarah every other weekend. There was no way Grace would let him take Sarah and ignore her. He hadn't ever wanted her. If he took her now, it would probably be out of a sense of duty to his family.

Still, if Grace argued, if she didn't handle this situation with kid gloves, her reply could sound like an accusation and accusations only caused arguments. She did not want to argue. She wanted all this settled as quickly and amicably as possible.

"It's good that you want to be involved—"

Danny suddenly turned from the window and caught her gaze, but Grace couldn't read the expression in his eyes and fell silent. She didn't know what he was thinking because she didn't know him. Not at all. She hadn't worked with him long enough to even know him as a boss. With Orlando he had been fun and funny. But when she'd told him about being pregnant he'd been hard, cold, unyielding. As far as she knew he had two personalities. A good guy and a bad guy and she had a sneaking suspicion few people saw the good guy.

"I want my daughter to live with me."

"Live with you?" *Grace* would be the one getting a visit every other Saturday afternoon? He had to be joking. Or insane.

"I've got money enough and clout enough that if I take you to court I'll end up with custody."

Grace gaped at him. It had been difficult to bring her child to meet him. As far as she was concerned, he could have stayed out of their lives forever. She was only here for Sarah's sake. Trying to grasp that he wanted to take Sarah away from her was staggering. Could his money really put Grace in a position where she'd be forced to hand over her innocent, defenseless baby daughter to a complete stranger? A man who didn't even want her?

She pulled in a breath and said, "That's ridiculous."

"Not really. When I retire, the option to take over Carson Services will be Sarah's. She'll need to be prepared. Only I can prepare her."

"But your son—"

"Never wanted the job. It falls to Sarah."

Overwhelmed, Grace shook her head. "This is too much in one day. I never even considered the possibility that you wanted to know I'd had a baby. Yet the day you find out, you're suddenly demanding custody."

"I don't have any other choice."

Grace sat in stunned silence. The whole hell of it was he didn't want Sarah. He wasn't asking for any reason except to fulfill a duty. Which was just wonderful. Grace would lose the baby she adored to a man who didn't want her, a man who intended to *train* her for a job. Not to love and nurture her, but to assure there was someone to take over the family business.

The injustice of it suffocated Grace at the same time that she understood it. Danny might not want Sarah, but he had a responsibility to her and to his family.

She wondered if he really needed to live with Sarah to teach her, then unexpectedly understood his side again. Preparing to take over a family fortune required more than a formal education. It required knowledge of family history and traditions. It required social graces. It required building social relationships.

All of which Grace didn't have. Sarah had to live with him at least part of the time.

Part of the time.

Suddenly inspired, Grace said, "You know what? I think I have a compromise."

"I don't compromise."

No kidding.

"Okay, then maybe what I have is a deal to propose."

His eyes narrowed ominously. "I don't need a deal, either."

"Well, listen anyway. The problem I see is that you don't know Sarah—"

"Living together will take care of that."

"Just listen. You don't know Sarah. I don't think you really want her. You're asking for custody out of a sense of duty and responsibility not to her but to your family, and, as bad as it is for my cause, I understand it. But as Sarah's mother I can't let you take my baby when you don't want her. So what I'm going to propose is that you come to live with Sarah and me for the next two weeks."

His face scrunched in confusion. "How exactly would that help?"

"If nothing else, in two weeks, I'll get to know you and you'll get to know her. Especially since I don't have a housekeeper or nanny. You and I will be the ones to care for her."

His shrewd brown eyes studied her, as if he were

trying to think of the catch. Since there was no catch, Grace continued.

"The deal is if you can spend two weeks with us, learning to care for her, and if at the end of that two weeks I feel comfortable with you having her, I won't contest *shared* custody. Week about. I get her one week. You have her the next. That way, as she gets older, you can schedule the functions you think she needs to be involved in, and I won't have to give her over to you permanently."

Danny shook his head. "Grace—"

"I won't give her over to you permanently. Not for any reason. Not any way. The best you'll get from me is week about and only if I believe you can handle her."

"You're not in a position to name terms," Danny said, shaking his head. "I can beat you in court."

"And then what?" Grace asked barely holding onto her temper. This time yesterday he didn't know he had a daughter. This time last year he didn't want to even hear Grace was pregnant. He couldn't expect her to hand over their child. She'd spend every cent of money she had before she'd recklessly hand over her baby to a man who didn't want Sarah, a man who probably would keep his distance and never love her.

"Say you do beat me in court. What are you going to do? Pass off your daughter's care to nannies, and let her be raised by a stranger when she could be spending that time with her mother? Is that your idea of grooming her? Showing her how to walk all over people?"

He ran his hand along the back of his neck.

She had him. They might not have spent much time

together, but she'd noticed that when he rubbed the back of his neck, he was thinking.

"It sure as hell isn't my idea of how to teach her," Grace said quietly, calming down so he would, too. "If nothing else, admit you need some time to adjust to being her dad."

He sighed. "You want *two* weeks?"

"If you can't handle her for two weeks, how do you expect to have her permanently?"

Danny said nothing and Grace retraced her argument, trying to figure out why two weeks made him hesitate. A person who wanted full custody couldn't object to a mere two-week stay with the same baby he was trying to get custody of —

Unless he wasn't worried about two weeks with Sarah as much as he was worried about two weeks with Grace. The last time they'd spent three *days* together they'd ended up in bed.

The air suddenly filled with electricity, so much that Grace could almost see the crackles and sparks. Memories—not of his accusations when she told him she was pregnant, but his soft caresses that Sunday night and Monday morning—flooded her mind and the attraction she'd felt the weekend they'd spent together returned full force.

But she didn't want it. She did not want to be attracted to this man. He'd come right out and said he didn't want a relationship with her. Plus, he had clout that she didn't have. Grace needed all her facilities to fight for Sarah's interests. She couldn't risk that he'd push her around in court the way he'd steamrolled her when she told him she was pregnant.

The reminder of how he'd kicked her out of his office without hearing her out was all she needed. Her chin came up. Her spine stiffened. She would never, ever trust him again. She would never give in to the attraction again.

"You're perfectly safe with me. Our time together was a mistake. I wouldn't even speak to you were it not for Sarah."

He remained silent so long that Grace sighed with disgust. He hadn't had a clue how painful his words had been to her. He hadn't cared that she could have misinterpreted everything he'd said and drawn the conclusion that he'd had his fun with her but she wasn't good enough to really love. He'd been so wrapped up in his own wants and needs that he never considered hers.

Or anyone's as far as Grace knew.

Another reason to stay the hell away from him.

"I mean it, Danny. I want nothing to do with you and will fight tooth and nail before I let you take Sarah even for weekends if only because you're a virtual stranger."

Obviously controlling his anger, he looked at the ceiling then back at her. "If I spend two weeks with you and the baby you won't contest shared custody," he said, repeating what he believed to be their arrangement.

"*If* by the end of those two weeks I believe you'll be good to Sarah."

Sarah had stopped sucking. Grace glanced down to see the baby had fallen asleep in her arms. "If you wish, we can have our lawyers draw up papers."

"Oh, I *will* have my lawyer write an agreement."

"Great. Once we get it signed we can start."

"You'll have it tonight. Do you have an e-mail address?"

"Yes."

"Watch your computer. You'll have the agreement before you go to bed. You can e-mail me directions to your house and I'll be there tomorrow."

CHAPTER FIVE

WHEN GRACE received Danny's e-mail with their agreement as an attachment, she realized that no matter how simple and straightforward, she couldn't sign any legal document without the advice of counsel. She replied saying she wanted her own lawyer to review the agreement before she signed it, expecting him to be angry at the delay. Instead he was surprisingly accommodating of her request.

She spoke with a lawyer Monday morning, who gave her the go-ahead to sign, and e-mailed Danny that she had executed the agreement and he could sign it that evening when he arrived at her house.

Busy at work, she didn't give Danny or the agreement another thought until she walked into the foyer of her little bungalow and saw something she hadn't considered.

The downstairs of her house had an open floor plan. Pale orange ceramic tile ran from the foyer to the back door. An oatmeal-colored Berber area rug sat beneath the burnt-orange tweed sofa and the matching love seat, delineating that space. Similarly the tan, brown and black print rug beneath the oak table and chairs marked off the dining area. A black-and-tan granite-topped breakfast bar separated the living room from the kitchen, but because there were no cabinets above it, people in the kitchen were clearly visible from any point downstairs.

Grace wasn't afraid that Danny wouldn't like her home. She didn't give a damn if he liked it or not. What troubled her was that with the exception of the two bedrooms, both upstairs, there was nowhere to hide. Anytime they were downstairs they would technically be together.

"Well, Sarah," she said, sliding the baby out of her carrier seat and giving her a quick kiss on the cheek. In her yellow one-piece outfit, Sarah looked like a ray of sunshine. "I guess it's too late to worry about that now."

As the words came out of her mouth, the doorbell rang, and Grace winced. If that was Danny, it really was too late to worry about the close quarters of her house now.

Angling the baby on her hip, Grace walked to the door and opened it. Danny stood on her small porch, holding a garment bag, with a duffel bag sitting beside his feet. Dressed in jeans and a loose-fitting sport shirt, he looked comfortable and relaxed, reminding her of their time together at his beach house.

A sudden avalanche of emotion overtook her. She had really fallen hard for him that weekend. Not just because he was sexy, though he was. He had an air of power and strength that—combined with his shiny black hair, piercing black eyes and fabulous body—

made him one of the sexiest men Grace had ever met. Staring into his eyes, she remembered the way he made love to her. She remembered their pillow talk and their one phone conversation. He had definitely felt something for her that weekend, too, but in the one short week he was out of town he'd lost it. He hadn't believed her when she told him she was pregnant. He'd kicked her out of his office. And now they were here. Fighting over custody of a baby he hadn't wanted.

"This house doesn't look big enough for two people, let alone three."

"It's got more space than you think," Grace said, opening the door a little wider so he could enter, as she reminded herself she had to do this because she couldn't beat him in court. "It looks like a ranch, but it isn't. There are two bedrooms upstairs."

"Yeah, they're probably no bigger than closets."

Grace told herself she could do this. She'd dealt with grouchy Danny every time she'd spoken to him— except for that one weekend. The person she'd met that weekend was more likely the exception and grouchy Danny was the rule. She wasn't about to let their two weeks begin with her apologizing.

Ignoring his closet comment, she said, "Let's take your bags upstairs and get them out of the way."

Grace turned and began walking up the steps, and, following after her, Danny got a flashback of following her up the steps of his beach house. It intensified when he glanced down at the steps to avoid looking at her shapely legs. The memory was so clear it made him dizzy, as if he were stepping back in time.

But he wasn't. They were here and now, fifteen months later. She'd had his child. She might have done it without him, but ultimately she'd brought the baby to him. And why not? As far as Grace knew little Sarah could inherit a fortune—even before Danny was dead if she became the CEO of Carson Services when Danny retired.

He didn't want even a portion of the family fortune to go to an opportunist, but his threat of taking Grace to court to get full custody had been empty. An attempt to pressure her into giving him their daughter. Then Grace had come up with a compromise and to Danny's surprise it really did suit him. He could train Sarah without paying off her mother.

Plus, he no longer had the worry that a custody battle gave her reason to dig into his past.

All he had to do was spend two weeks with Grace, a woman who he believed tricked him.

At the top of the steps, Grace turned to the right, opened a door, and stepped back so he could enter the room. To his surprise, Grace was correct, the bedroom was more spacious than he'd thought from the outward appearance of the house. Even with a double bed in the center of the room, a knotty pine armoire and dresser, and a small desk in the corner, there was plenty of space to walk.

He hesitantly said, "This is nice."

"We have to share the bathroom."

He faced her. She'd taken a few steps into the room, as if wanting to be available to answer questions, but not exactly thrilled to be in the same room with him. Especially not a bedroom.

Her soft voice triggered another batch of beach house memories. Grace telling him to promote someone else. Grace looking like an angel in front of the upstairs widows. Grace ready to accept his kiss…

He shoved the memories out of his brain, reminding himself that woman probably didn't exist. "I'll keep my things in a shaving kit. I won't take up any room."

She turned away from him with a shrug. Walking to the door, she said, "It doesn't matter one way or the other to me."

He couldn't tell if she intended to insult him or prove to him that his being there had no meaning to her beyond their reaching an accord about custody, but the indifference he heard in her voice was just fine with him. He didn't want to be involved with her any more than she wanted to be involved with him.

Which should make for a fabulous two weeks.

He tossed his duffel bag on the bed and walked the garment bag to the closet before going downstairs. At the bottom of the steps, he realized that the entire first floor of the house was open. He could see Grace puttering in the compact kitchen and Sarah swinging contentedly in the baby swing sitting in the space between the dining area and living room.

Walking to the kitchen, he said, "Anything I can help you with?"

"You're here for Sarah. So why don't you amuse her, while I make dinner?"

"Okay." Her cool tone of voice didn't affect him because she was correct. He was here for Sarah. Not for Grace. Not to make small talk or plans or, God forbid, even to become friendly.

He glanced at the cooing baby. A trip to the department store that morning to arrange for baby furniture to be delivered to his house had shown him just how behind the times he had become in the nine years that had passed since Cory was a baby. Playpens were now play yards. Car seats had become downright challenging. He didn't have to be a genius to know that if the equipment had changed, so had the rules. He wouldn't do anything with Sarah without asking.

"Should I take her out of the seat?"

Pulling a salad bowl from a cabinet, Grace said, "Not when she's happy. Just sit on the floor in front of her and chat."

Chat. With a baby. He'd tried that the day Grace brought Sarah to his house and hadn't known what to say. Obviously he had to think of something to talk about other than investing. But he wasn't sitting on the floor. After a quick look around, he grabbed one of the oak ladder-back chairs from the table in the dining room section and set it in front of the swing.

"Hey, Sarah."

She pulled the blue plastic teething ring from her mouth and cooed at him. He smiled and settled more comfortably on the chair as he studied her, trying to think of something to say. Nothing came. She gurgled contently as she waved her arms, sending the scent of baby powder through the air to his nose. That brought a burst of memories of Cory.

He'd been so proud of that kid. So smitten. So enamored with the fun of having a baby that he'd thought his life was perfect. Then Cory had shown artistic ability and Lydia wanted to send him to special school. Danny had thought she was jumping the gun, making a decision that didn't need to be made until Cory was older.

Taking a breath, Danny forced himself back to the present. He had to stop thinking of Cory. He had to focus on Sarah. He had to create an amicable relationship so their time together would be happy and not a horrible strain.

Then he noticed that the one-piece yellow thing she wore made her hair appear reddish brown. "I think somebody's going to be a redhead."

The baby gooed. Danny smiled. Curious, he turned toward the kitchen. "My parents are French and English. So I don't think the red hair comes from my side of the family. How about yours?"

Grace grudgingly said, "Both of my parents are Scottish."

"Well, that explains it."

Danny's comment fell on total silence. Though he was here for Sarah, he and Grace had two long weeks to spend together. He might not want to be her friend, but he didn't want to be miserable, either. Studying Grace as she ripped lettuce and tossed it into a bowl, he swore he could see waves of anger emanate from her.

It might have been her idea to share custody, but she clearly didn't want to spend two weeks with him any more than he wanted to spend two weeks with her. He'd forced her hand with the threat of taking her baby away.

Taking her baby away.

He hadn't really looked at what he was doing from her perspective and suddenly realized how selfish he must seem to her.

"Had I gone for full custody, I wouldn't have shut you out of her life completely."

"No, but you would have demanded that she live with you and I'd be the one with visitation."

She walked over to him and displayed a plate with two steaks. "I'm going to the back deck to the grill." She waited a heartbeat, then said, "You're not afraid to be alone with her, are you?"

As if any man would ever admit to being afraid of anything. "No. But I'm guessing you're a better choice to stay inside with her, which means I should grill the steaks."

"Great." She handed him the plate. "I'll finish the salad."

She pivoted and returned to the kitchen without waiting for his reply. Danny rose from his seat and walked out to the deck. He agreed with her nonconversation policy. There was no point in talking. She didn't like him. And, well, frankly, he didn't like her.

He dropped the plate of steaks on a small table and set the temperature on the grill. Still, whether he agreed with her or not, not talking guaranteed that the next two weeks would be two of the longest of his life. Torture really. Maybe payback for his not believing her? He slapped the steaks on the grill rack.

That was probably it. Payback. But what Grace didn't realize was that the way she treated him was also proof that she wasn't the sweet innocent she'd pretended to be.

He almost laughed. What a mess. All because he couldn't keep his hands off a woman. He'd never make *that* mistake again.

He closed the lid and looked out over the expanse of backyard. Grace didn't have a huge space but what she had was well tended. Her bungalow was neat and clean, newly remodeled. Her yard was well kept. He hoped that was an indicator that Grace would take good care of Sarah during the weeks she had her.

He heard a giggle from inside the house. Turning, he saw he hadn't shut the French doors. He ambled over and was just about to push them closed when he heard Grace talking. "So, somebody needs to go upstairs and get a fresh diaper."

She lifted the baby from the swing and rubbed noses with her. "I swear, Sarah, there's got to be a better system."

The baby laughed. Danny sort of chuckled himself. A person would think that after all the generations of babies, somebody, somewhere would have thought of a better system than diapers.

"Let's take care of that. Then we'll feed you something yummy for dinner."

The baby giggled and cooed and Danny felt a quick

sting of conscience for worrying about Sarah when she was in Grace's care. Grace obviously loved the baby.

He took a quick breath. She might love the baby but there was a lot more to consider in child rearing than just love. Grace was on trial these next two weeks every bit as much as he was. He wouldn't be convinced she was a good mom, just because she was sweet. She wasn't sweet. As far as he knew she was a conniver. She could have seen the French doors were open and put on a show with the baby for him to see.

He closed the doors and checked the steaks. They were progressing nicely. He sat on one of the deck chairs. The thick red, yellow and tan striped padding felt good to his tired back and he let his eyelids droop. He didn't raise them again until he heard the French doors open.

"How's it going?" Grace asked quietly. Sarah sat on her forearm, once again chewing the blue teething ring.

Danny sat up. "Fine. I was just about to peek at the steaks." He poked and prodded the steaks, closed the lid and chucked Sarah under the chin. "You're just about the cutest kid in the world, aren't you?"

Sarah giggled and cooed and Grace regretted her decision to bring the baby with her when she checked on him. When she least expected it, he would say or do something that would remind her that she'd genuinely believed he was a nice, normal guy the weekend they'd spent at the beach house. Volunteering to help her in the kitchen when he first came downstairs hadn't been expected. His wanting to know Sarah's heritage had struck her as adorable. And now he looked perfectly natural, perfectly comfortable on her back deck.

But he was also here to convince Grace that he would be able to care for Sarah. Technically he was on good behavior. She refused to get sucked in again as she had at the beach house.

She turned to go back into the house, but he said, "Grace?" And every nerve ending she had went on red alert. He had a sexy quality to his voice that was magnified when he spoke softly. Of course, that took her back to their pillow talk the night they had slept together and that made her all quivery inside.

Scowling because she didn't want to like him and did want to let him know that if he thought he could charm her he was wrong, she faced him. "Yes?"

"You never told me how you wanted your steak."

Feeling embarrassment heat her cheeks, she quickly turned to the door again. "Medium is fine."

With that she walked into the house. She put Sarah in her high chair and rummaged through the cupboards for a jar of baby food, which she heated. By the time she was done feeding Sarah, had her face cleaned and the rubber teething ring back in her chubby hands, Danny brought in the steaks.

"Salad is on the counter," she said, as she laid plates and silverware on the table. "Could you bring that in, too?" Her new strategy was to put him to work before he could volunteer. This way, he wouldn't seem nice, he would only be following orders.

He did as she asked and they sat down at the table,

across from each other, just as they had been sitting that Sunday night at his beach house. She'd dressed up, hoping he would notice her. But tonight, on the trip upstairs to change Sarah's diaper, she'd put on her worst jeans, her ugliest T-shirt. What a difference fifteen months made.

"Your house is nice."

"Thank you."

Silence reigned for another minute, before Danny said, "So, did you buy it remodeled like this?"

She bit back a sigh, loath to tell him anything about herself. More than that, though, they'd discussed this that night at the beach house. He'd forgotten. So much for thinking she'd made any kind of impression on him

"It was a wreck when I bought it."

"Oh, so you did the remodeling—I mean with a contractor, right?"

"No. My cousin and I remodeled it." And she'd told him that, too.

He smiled. "Really?"

Grace rose from her seat. "You know what? I'm really not all that hungry and it's time for me to get Sarah bathed and ready for bed." She smiled stiffly. "If you'll excuse me."

Alone at the table Danny quietly finished his steak. If Grace was going to continually take Sarah and leave the room, maybe he shouldn't cancel tomorrow's dinner engagement? He drew in a breath, then expelled it quickly. He couldn't dodge or fudge this commitment. He wanted at least shared custody of his daughter, and Grace had handed him the way to get it without a custody battle that would result in her investigating his past and probably result in him losing all but scant visitation rights. So he couldn't leave. He had to be here every minute he could for the next two weeks.

The problem was he and Grace also had to be together. He'd thought they could be at least cordial, but this was what he got for his positive attitude. The silent treatment. Well, she could save herself the trouble if she intended to insult him. His ex-wife had been the ultimate professional when it came to the silent treatment. Grace would have to go a long way to match that.

But when he'd not only finished eating his dinner and stacking the dishes in the dishwasher and Grace still hadn't come downstairs, he wondered if maybe she couldn't give Lydia a tip or two in the silent treatment department. Angry, because the whole point of his being here was to spend time with his daughter, Danny stormed up the steps. He stopped outside Grace's bedroom door because it was ajar and what he saw compelled him to rethink everything.

Though Grace's bedroom was pretty, decorated in warm colors like reds, yellows and taupe, a big white crib, white changing table and two white dressers took up most of the space. Still, there was enough adult furniture pushed into the room's corners that Danny could almost envision how she probably had her room before the baby was born. When she met him, she had had a pretty house, a sanctuary bedroom and a budding career. When she got pregnant, she'd lost her job. When she actually had Sarah, most of her pretty house had become a nursery.

"Oh, now, you can't be sleepy yet."

Grace's soft voice drifted out into the hallway.

"You still need to spend some time with your daddy."

Danny swallowed when he heard himself referred to again as a daddy. He was only getting used to that.

"I know you're tired, but just stay awake long enough to say good-night."

She lifted Sarah from the changing table and brushed her cheek across the baby's little cheek. Mesmerized, Danny watched. He'd forgotten how stirring it was to watch a mother with her baby.

"Come on," Grace said, turning to the door. Danny jumped back, out of her line of vision.

Thinking fast, he leaped into his room and quickly closed the door. He counted to fifty, hoping that gave her enough time to get downstairs, then opened the door a crack and peered out into the hall. When he found it empty, he walked downstairs, too. Grace sat on the sofa, Sarah on her lap.

"Can I hold her before she goes to bed?"

"Sure."

She made a move to rise, but Danny stopped her. "I'll take her from your lap."

Grace nodded and Danny reached down to get Sarah. Lifting her, he let his eyes wander over to Grace and their gazes caught. Except now he knew why he was no longer dealing with the sweet, innocent woman he'd slept with at the beach house. Her life had changed so much that even if she hadn't tricked him, she couldn't be the same woman. She'd gotten pregnant to a stranger. He'd rejected her. She'd lost her job and was too sick to get another. She'd had her baby alone. Any of those would have toughened her. Made her cynical. Maybe even made her angry.

No. She was no longer the woman he knew from the beach house.

CHAPTER SIX

DANNY awakened to the sounds of the shower. Grace was up before him and already started on her day. He waited until the shower stopped, then listened for the sounds of the bathroom door opening before he got out of bed, slipped on a robe and grabbed his shaving kit.

In the hall he heard the melodious sounds of Grace's voice as she spoke to Sarah and laughed with her. He stopped. Her soft laughter took him back to their weekend at the beach house. He shook his head and walked into the bathroom. He had to stop remembering. As he'd realized last night, that Grace no longer existed. Plus, they had a child. Sarah's future was in their hands. He didn't take that responsibility lightly anymore.

After a quick shower, Danny dressed in a navy suit, ready for a long day of business meetings. He jogged down the stairs and was immediately enfolded in the scent of breakfast.

Walking to the small dining area, he said, "Good morning."

Grace breezed away from the table and strode into the kitchen. "Good morning."

Sarah grinned up at him toothlessly. He smiled down at her. "And how are you today?"

Sarah giggled. Danny took a seat at the table. Grace set a dish containing an omelet, two slices of toast and some applesauce in front of him. Suddenly her coolness made sense. He'd forced her to have their baby alone, yet she'd nonetheless suggested shared custody, allowing him into her home to give him the opportunity to prove himself. Even if the Grace who'd seduced him that night no longer existed, the woman who'd taken her place had her sense of generosity. Even to her detriment. She wouldn't cheat him out of time with her daughter. Or use Sarah as a weapon. She was fair and it cost her.

Grace set her dish at the place opposite Danny and sat down. She immediately grabbed her napkin, opened it on her lap and picked up her fork.

Sarah shrieked.

Grace shook her head. "You already ate."

Sarah pounded her teething ring on the high chair tray.

"A tantrum will do you no good," Grace said to Sarah, but Danny was painfully aware that she didn't speak to him. She didn't even look at him.

His chest tightened. She'd been such a fun, bubbly, lively person. Now she was cautious and withdrawn. And he had done this to her.

Grace all but gobbled her breakfast. She noticed that Danny had become quiet as she drank a cup of coffee, but she didn't have time to care. She wasn't entirely sure she would care even if she had time. He'd basically accused her of lying. He clearly believed she'd tricked him. And if both of those weren't enough, he intended to take her child every other week. She didn't want to be his friend. He was only in her house because she couldn't risk that he'd get full custody, and she also wouldn't risk her child's happiness with a grouch. So he was here to prove himself. She didn't have to entertain him.

He was lucky she'd made him breakfast. That was why she was late, and rushing, so if he expected a little morning chitchat, that was his problem.

Having eaten enough food to sustain herself until lunch, Grace rose from her seat and took her dish to the kitchen. To her surprise Danny was right behind her when she turned from the dishwasher. Her heart thudded in her chest, half from surprise, half from being so close to him. He radiated warmth or energy, or something, that made being near him intoxicating. And trouble. His being irresistible was what had caused her to let her guard down in the first place.

He handed her his plate, though most of his food hadn't been eaten.

She took a quick gulp of air to try to rid herself of the breathless feeling and looked up at him. His eyes mirrored an emotion she couldn't quite read, except that he was unsure of what he was supposed to be doing.

"I'm rushing because I'm late. You can stay and finish. Just rinse your plate when you're through and put it in the dishwasher."

"I've had enough," Danny said and as Grace turned away from the dishwasher she saw him glance around her small kitchen. "Since I'm the boss I don't have to worry about being late, so if you'd like I could clean up in here."

In his neat navy blue suit, white shirt and blue print tie, he might look like the guy who ran Carson Services, but he behaved like the Danny Grace had met at the beach house, and that wasn't right. Being attracted to him wasn't right. Even being friendly wasn't right, if only because they were on opposite ends of a custody battle.

"No, thank you," she coolly replied. "It will take me only a minute or two to wipe the skillet and stove. You go on ahead. I'm fine."

"Grace," he said with a chuckle. "It's not a big deal."

"Really?" Try as she might, she couldn't keep the sarcasm out of her voice. "I'm surprised a rich guy like you even knows how to clean a skillet."

He laughed. The sound danced along her nerve endings, reminding her again of how he'd been the night they'd made love. She fought the happy memories by recalling the scene in his office. The one where he'd called her pregnancy a scheme.

"I couldn't exactly take a maid to university. My parents might have gotten me an apartment, but unless I wanted to live in squalor I had to do at least a little straightening up."

Grace felt herself softening to him and squeezed her eyes shut. It was much easier dealing with mean Danny. No expectations were better than unmet expectations.

Opening her eyes, she faced him. "Look, I don't want you to be nice to me. I don't need you to be nice."

"Helping clean up isn't nice. It's common courtesy."

"Well, save it. You're here to prove yourself with Sarah. And you did fine this morning just by saying good morning. You noticed her. You didn't ignore her. You're on the right track."

"I'm not going to let you wait on me while I'm here."

Grace removed her apron and set it on the counter. She didn't have time or the inclination to argue. She also couldn't give a damn what he did. That only tripped memories of a man she was absolutely positive didn't exist. She couldn't get into arguments that tempted her to believe otherwise.

"Fine. Dishcloths are in the bottom drawer."

She walked out of the kitchen and over to the high chair, where she lifted Sarah into her arms before she headed for the stairway.

But from the corner of her eye she could see Danny standing in the kitchen, plate in hand, watching her. He looked totally out of place and equally confused and Grace again fought against emotions she couldn't afford to have.

How could he make her feel like the one in the wrong when he had done such terrible things to her?

After a horrifically long day, Danny finally had ten minutes alone in his office. Though he tried to make a few phone calls before leaving he couldn't. Being with Grace at her house and yet not really being with Grace was driving him crazy. He could not live with someone for two whole weeks who barely spoke to him. Not that he wanted lively conversation, but he couldn't handle being ignored, either. Plus, if they didn't at least discuss Sarah and her care, especially her likes and dislikes, how were these two weeks supposed to prove to Grace that she could relax when Sarah was with him?

Knowing it wouldn't help matters if he were late for dinner that night, Danny stuffed a few files into a briefcase and left early. At her front door, he hesitated. He felt so ill at ease just walking inside that he should ring the bell. But he was living here. The next two weeks this was his home. And maybe walking in would jar Grace into realizing she had to deal with him.

He opened the door and saw Grace on the floor with Sarah, playing peekaboo.

"Hey."

Sarah squealed her delight at seeing him. Grace glanced over. "Hey."

He didn't smell anything cooking and finally, finally saw a golden opportunity. "I was thinking this afternoon that things might go easier if we just went out to dinner." He paused, but she didn't say anything. "On me, of course."

She sighed, lifted Sarah into her arms and rose from the floor. "It's not practical to go out to a restaurant with a baby every night." She walked into the kitchen, Sarah on her hip.

With Grace's reply ringing in his head, Danny looked around again. Two bears sat on the sofa. A baby swing was angled in such a way that the baby inside could be seen from the kitchen, dining room or living room. A high chair sat by the dining table. Blocks were stacked on the buffet. The room smelled of baby powder.

He remembered this now. For the first few years of a baby's life everything revolved around the baby. That had been a difficult enough adjustment for a married couple. But it had to be all-consuming for a single mom. Not just because she didn't have assistance with Sarah, but because it affected everything.

He walked into the kitchen. "Can I help with dinner?"

She pulled a package of hamburger from the refrigerator. "Do you want to grill the hamburgers?"

Eager to do his share, Danny said, "Sure."

He reached for the hamburger, but Grace pointed at his jacket and tie. "You can't cook in that."

He grimaced. "Right."

After changing into jeans and a T-shirt, he took the hamburger from the refrigerator and headed for the back deck and the grill. Grace was nowhere around, but he assumed she and the baby were in her room. Maybe because the baby needed a diaper change.

Gazing out over the short backyard Danny studied the houses near Grace's. Realizing none was as well kept as hers, he remembered her telling him about remodeling her home the night they spent at his beach house. That was why her comments about wanting to be rich hadn't struck him oddly that night. He knew she was a hard worker. But three weeks later when she told him she was pregnant, he'd forgotten how eager she was to earn her way in life. He only remembered that she'd wanted to be rich and he'd assumed the worst.

He'd seduced her, left her for a week, said he didn't want to see her again when he returned, refused to believe her when she told him she was pregnant and then threatened to file for full custody of their baby. While he'd acted on inaccurate "interpretations" of things she'd done, he'd given her five very real reasons to hate him.

It was no wonder she was cool to him. He'd not only misjudged her. He'd behaved like a horrible person.

The sound of a car pulling into her driveway brought him out of his thoughts. He strode to the far end of the deck and glanced around the side of the house just in time to see Grace pulling Sarah from the car seat. With a grocery bag hooked over her arm and Sarah perched on the other, she walked, head down, into the house.

Danny's heart squeezed in his chest. Would he ever stop hurting people?

Grace stepped into her house at the same time that Danny walked in from the deck. "Where did you go?"

"I needed milk and hamburger buns." Carrying Sarah, she went to the kitchen to deposit her purchases.

Danny grabbed the gallon jug that dangled from her hand and put it in the refrigerator. "I could have gone to the store."

"Well, I did."

He sighed. "Grace, I want to help but I can't do things that I don't know need done."

"I didn't ask you to do anything."

But even as the words were coming out of her mouth, Grace regretted them. She slid Sarah into the high chair and turned to face Danny. He might be a difficult person, but she wasn't. And she refused to let him turn her into one.

"Here's the deal. I'm accustomed to being on my own. There's no point in breaking that habit because you'll only be here for another twelve days. So don't worry about it. Okay?"

He nodded, but he kept looking at her oddly as if she'd just discovered the secret to life. He continued to steal peeks at her all through dinner, making her nervous enough that she chattered to Sarah as they ate their hamburgers and salads, if only to bring some sound into the room.

When she could legitimately slip away to feed Sarah a bottle and put her to bed, she felt as if she were escaping a prison. She extended her alone time with a long, soothing shower, but rather than slip into her usual nightgown and robe she put on sweatpants and a T-shirt and shuffled downstairs to watch a little TV to unwind before trying to sleep.

She had just turned off all the lights and settled on the sofa with a cup of cocoa, when Danny came down the steps.

Seeing her curled up on the couch, he paused. "Sorry."

He pivoted to go back upstairs and Grace said, "Wait." She didn't want to be his friend. She didn't want to like him. She most certainly didn't want to get romantically involved with him. But she couldn't take the silence anymore and she suspected he couldn't, either.

"You don't have to leave. For the next two weeks this is your home. We might as well get accustomed to each other."

At first he hesitated, but then he slowly made his way down the steps and into the sitting area.

"Would you like some cocoa?"

As he lowered himself to the love seat, he chuckled softly. "I haven't had cocoa in—"

He stopped. Grace suspected that the last time he'd had cocoa it had been with his son, but she was also tired of tiptoeing around his life. He'd told her very little about himself the night they had dinner at the beach house and she'd not pushed him. But if she had to accept him into her house and Sarah's life, then he had to accept her into his. They couldn't pretend his other life didn't exist.

"In?" Grace prompted, forcing him to talk about his son.

"In years." He took a breath and caught her gaze. "Since I had cocoa with my son."

The words hung in the room. Danny kept his gaze locked with Grace's, as if daring her to go further. But she had no intention of delving into every corner of his world. She only wanted them to begin having normal conversations, so the tension between them would ease.

"See. We can talk about both of your children." She rose from the sofa. "Let me make you a cup of cocoa."

Without waiting for his reply, she walked into the kitchen, pulled a small pot from the cupboard by the stove and set it on a burner. Danny lowered himself to one of the stools by the counter, reminding Grace of how she had sat at the beach house bar while he poured himself a glass of Scotch.

Danny suddenly bounced from the seat, as if he'd had the memory, too, and didn't want it. He strode into the kitchen and reached for the refrigerator door handle. "I'll help you."

Removing the cocoa from a cupboard, Grace turned so quickly that she and Danny nearly ran into each other in the compact kitchen.

He caught her elbows to steady her, and tingles of awareness skipped along her skin. This close she could feel the heat of his body. Memories of making love, of how different he had been that night and how happy she had been, flipped through her brain. The sizzle between them was so intense she suddenly wondered what might have happened if they hadn't made love that night. Would the nice guy she'd met at the beach house have pursued her? Would he have remained nice? Would they have discovered differences and gone their separate ways or lived happily ever after?

Pulling her arms away, she turned toward the stove. What might have been wasn't an issue. If she thought about what might have been for too long she might get starry-eyed again and that would be insane. The guy had hurt her and now he wanted her child. She wouldn't be reckless with him again.

"Hand me the milk."

He did.

"Thanks." Exaggerating the task of pouring it into the pan so she didn't have to look at him, she said, "How are things at Carson Services?"

He walked back to the counter, but didn't sit. Instead he leaned against it. "Fine."

"How's Orlando?"

Danny laughed. "Great. He's a dream client. Because he does his homework, we're always on the same page when I suggest he move his money."

"That's so good to hear. I liked him."

"He's asked about you."

Dumping three scoops of cocoa on top of the milk, she grimaced. "What did you tell him?"

Danny shifted uncomfortably. "That you'd moved on."

She heard the stirring of guilt in his voice. Though part of her found it fitting, she couldn't pretend she was innocent. She'd recognized from the beginning that losing her job was one of the potential consequences of a failed relationship between them. So she wouldn't pretend. She would discuss this like an adult.

She faced him. "So you told him the truth."

"Excuse me?"

"What you told him was the truth. I *had* moved on."

He barked a laugh. "Yeah."

Grace walked over to him and stood in front of him, holding his gaze. "We won't survive twelve more days of living together if we don't admit here and now that we both made mistakes that weekend. We don't need to dissect our sleeping together and place blame. But we do need to admit that we *both* made mistakes."

"Okay."

"It is okay because we both moved on."

"Bet you wish you had stayed moved on."

She might be willing to agree to be polite and even friendly, but she didn't intend to discuss nebulous things like regrets. So she fell back on humor to get her out of the conversation. Batting her hand in dismissal, she said, "Nah. What fun is having a nice, quiet life with no one pestering you for custody of your child?"

He laughed again. She turned to leave, but he caught her fingers and stopped her. Her gaze swung back to his.

"You're one of only a few people who make me laugh."

Memory thrummed through her. Her being able to make him laugh had been their first connection. But the touch of his fingers reminded her that they'd taken that connection so much further that night. She remembered the way his hands had skimmed her body, remembered how he'd held her, remembered the intensity of the fire of passion between them.

But in the end, passion had failed them. The only thing they had between them now was Sarah. And everything they did had to be for Sarah.

Grace cleared her throat and stepped back. "We'll work on getting you to laugh more often for Sarah." She pulled her hand away from his, walked to the stove and poured Danny's cocoa into a mug. "So what do you like to watch?"

"Watch?"

"On TV."

He took the mug she handed to him. "Actually I don't watch TV."

"Then you're in for a treat because you get to watch everything I like."

That made him laugh again, and Grace's heart lightened before she could stop it, just as it had their weekend together. But she reminded herself that things at the beach house had not turned out well. And she didn't intend to make the same mistake twice. He needed to be comfortable and relaxed for Sarah. She and Danny also needed to be reasonably decent to each other to share custody. But that was all the further she could let things between them go.

They spent two hours watching crime dramas on television. Danny was oddly amused by them. The conversation remained neutral, quiet, until at the end of the second show the eleven o'clock news was announced and Grace said she was going to bed.

"Ripped from the headline is right," he said, when Grace hit the off button on the remote and rose from the sofa. "That program couldn't have been more specific unless they'd named names."

"That's the show's gimmick. The writers take actual situations and fictionalize them. It's a way to give curious, gossip-hungry viewers a chance to see what might have happened, and how it would play out in court."

Danny said, "Right," then followed her up the stairs. In the little hallway between their closed bedroom doors, Danny put his hand on his doorknob, but he couldn't quite open the door. It didn't seem right to leave her just yet. And that spurred another beach house memory. He hadn't wanted to leave her after he'd given her her bonus. He'd tried to ignore the feeling, but Grace had followed him down to the bar in his great room.

That made him smile. The hall in which they stood was far from great. It was a little square. Only a bit wider than the bar that had separated them at the beach house. He'd closed that gap by leaning forward and kissing her, and he'd experienced one of the most wonderful nights of his life.

And he'd ruined even the pleasant memories he could hold onto and enjoy by not believing her. Not appreciating her.

"Thanks for the cocoa."

She faced him with a smile. "You're welcome."

He took a step away from his door and toward hers. He might not have appreciated her the weekend at the beach house, but tonight he was beginning to understand that she probably had been the woman he'd believed her to be when he seduced her. Everything that had happened between them was his fault. Especially their misunderstandings.

He caught her gaze. "I'm glad you moved on."

He took another step toward her, catching her hand and lifting it, studying the smooth skin, her delicate fingers. He recalled her fingers skimming his back, tunneling through his hair, driving him crazy with desire, and felt it all again, as if it were yesterday.

"I'm a lot stronger than I look."

Her words came out as a breathy whisper. The same force of attraction that swam through his veins seemed to be affecting her. In the quiet house, the only sound Danny heard was the pounding of his heart. The only thought in his mind was that he should kiss her.

Slowly, holding her gaze, watching for reaction, he lowered his head. Closing his eyes, he touched his lips to hers. They were smooth and sweet, just as he remembered. Warmth and familiarity collided with sexual hunger that would have happily overruled common sense. Their chemistry caused him to forget everything except how much he wanted her. How happy she made him. How natural it was to hold her.

But just when he would have deepened the kiss, she stepped away.

"This is what got us into trouble the last time." She caught his gaze. "Good night, Danny."

And before he could form the words to stop her, she was behind her closed bedroom door.

CHAPTER SEVEN

DANNY awoke feeling oddly refreshed. He opened his eyes, saw the sunny yellow bedroom around him and was disoriented until he remembered he was living with Grace.

Grace.

He'd kissed her, but she'd reminded him that was what had gotten them into trouble the last time. And he didn't think she was talking about creating Sarah. Sarah wasn't trouble. Sarah was a joy. Their "trouble" was that they had slept together when they didn't know each other, which was why he hadn't trusted her enough to continue the relationship, and why he hadn't believed Grace when she told him she was pregnant. He'd thought she was lying to him. Tricking him. Because he didn't know her well enough to realize Grace would never do something like that.

He now knew his accusations were the product of an overly suspicious mind, but he also had to admit to himself that he hadn't changed much from the man who had dismissed her as a liar. Yes, he'd gotten past the tragedies of his life and to the outside world he appeared normal. And he really could be normal at work, normal with friends, normal with a woman only looking for an evening of entertainment. But his divorce had soured him on commitment. He wasn't marriage material. He wasn't even a good date for anyone who wanted anything other than a fun night out or no-strings-attached sex. Forget about being the right guy for someone as wonderful as Grace. She deserved better. Even he knew it.

She needed a husband. A mate. Someone to share her life. He was not that guy.

He rolled out of bed and tugged on his robe. But once the slash belt was secured, he stopped again. He'd nearly forgotten he was sharing a bathroom.

Sharing a bathroom.

Watching TV.

And happy.

How long had it been since he could say he was happy? Years. He'd accustomed himself to settling for surface emotions, convinced that if he loved anything, life would yank it away. But though he might not believe he could make a commitment to a woman, living with Grace made him consider that he could love Sarah and he could be a real dad. Especially since Grace was kind enough, honest enough, fair enough that she was willing to share custody. Not as adversaries, but as two friends. Both having the best interests of their little girl at heart. And without a hearing that would air his less-than-perfect past.

He grabbed his shaving kit, opened his bedroom door and glanced down the short hall. The bathroom door was open and Grace wasn't anywhere to be seen. Good. He didn't want to bump into Grace dressed only in a robe. As she'd reminded him last night, kissing— or more appropriately runaway emotions and hormones—had gotten them into trouble the last time. He wasn't going to make the same mistake twice. Getting romantically involved had cost them. He'd lost a good employee and someone who probably would have turned into a friend.

And he'd hurt her.

He wouldn't let himself forget that. He also wouldn't let himself hurt her again. He could say that with absolute certainty because he wouldn't get involved with her again. That was a promise he was making to himself.

He showered and shaved and was back in his bedroom before he heard the sound of Grace's alarm. Removing a suit from the garment bag he'd hung in the closet, he heard Sarah's wailing and Grace's words of comfort. He put the suit back in the closet, and yanked on jeans and a T-shirt, listening to Grace soothing Sarah as she carried her downstairs. He heard Grace quietly return upstairs and knew that the lack of crying meant Sarah was sucking her bottle.

He listened for the sound of Grace's door closing and then sneaked downstairs. It had been years since he'd made his "world famous" blueberry pancakes, but if anybody ever deserved a little treat, it was Grace.

After taking a last peek to be sure her black skirt and print blouse were in the proper position, Grace shifted away from her full-length mirror to lift already-dressed Sarah from her crib. But as she turned, the scent of something sweet stopped her.

Whatever it was it smelled like pure heaven.

Her mouth watered.

She grabbed Sarah and rushed down the steps. In the kitchen, dressed in jeans and a T-shirt and wearing a bib apron, stood Danny.

"What is that smell?"

He turned with a smile. "Pancakes. My one and only specialty."

"If they taste as good as they smell, they are absolutely your specialty."

"Oh, they do."

The ringing endorsement—combined with the growling of Grace's tummy—had her scampering into the dining area. She slid Sarah into her high chair and went to the kitchen to retrieve plates from the cupboard. "More stuff you learned while at school?"

He winced. "Not really. These are the only thing I can cook. Unless you count canned soup and fried eggs."

Avoiding her eyes, he set two fluffy blueberry pancakes on each of the two plates she held. Grace took them to the table. She set her dish at the seat beside the high chair and the second across the table from her.

The night before he'd kissed her and just the memory of that brought a warm fuzzy somersault feeling to her empty tummy. She hadn't let the kiss go too far. But there was something between them.

Something special. Something sharp and sexual. It wasn't something that would go away with the press of a button, or just because it complicated things. And today he'd made her breakfast. Though she appreciated it, she also knew she had to tread lightly. She didn't want to get involved with him again and he was tempting her.

Danny brought the syrup to the table and sat across from her. "I think there are some things you and I need to discuss."

Her stomach flip-flopped again. The last thing she wanted was to talk about their one-night stand. Or whatever it was that had happened between them. But disliking him hadn't worked to keep them apart. So maybe it was best to talk?

"Okay."

He took a breath. "All right. Here's the deal. That kiss last night was wrong and I don't want you to have to worry about it happening again."

She looked across the table at him, her heart in her throat, and praying her eyes weren't revealing the pain that brought. She also didn't think getting involved was a good idea, but he hadn't needed to say the words.

"The truth is I know you deserve better than me."

Grace blinked. That wasn't at all what she was expecting and she had absolutely no idea how to reply.

"The night we slept together, I was going through a bad time," he said, glancing down at his pancake before catching her gaze again. "Not that that makes what happened right, but I think it might help you to understand that now that I'm past those personal problems, I can see I misjudged you and I'm sorrier than I can ever say."

Grace took a breath. Once again he was talking about himself, but not really about anything. Still his apology was a big step for them. "Okay."

"Okay you understand or okay you accept my apology?"

She took another breath. Her gut reaction was to accept his apology, but she simply didn't trust him. He had a powerful personality. He might say that she needn't worry about him kissing her again, but she didn't believe either of them could say that with absolute certainty. There was something between them. Chemistry, probably. Hormones that didn't listen to reason. She was afraid that if she accepted his apology and told him she understood it would open the door to things she couldn't control. Things neither one of them could control.

Before she could answer, Danny said, "I hate excuses for bad behavior, but sometimes there are valid reasons people do all the wrong things." He took a breath. "Because that weekend was the two-year anniversary of my son's death, I wasn't myself."

Grace blinked. "What?"

"Cory had died two years before. Six months after his accident my wife and I divorced. I spent the next year and a half just going through the motions of living."

Shocked into silence, Grace only stared at him.

"That weekend you reminded me of happiness." He combed his fingers through his hair. "I don't know.

Watching you with Orlando and hearing the two of you make jokes and have a good time, I remembered how it felt to be happy and I began to feel as if I were coming around." He caught her gaze. "You know…as if I were ready to live again."

Stuck in the dark place of trying to imagine the crushing blow of the death of a child and feeling overwhelmed at even the thought, Grace only nodded.

"But I'd always believed you and I had gone too far too fast by making love the very first weekend we really even spoke, and when I went away for that week of client hopping my doubts haunted me. I started imagining all kinds of reasons you'd sleep with me without really knowing me, and some of them weren't very flattering." He took a breath. "When you told me you were pregnant it just seemed as if every bad thing I had conjured had come true." He held her gaze steadily. "I was wrong and I am sorry."

Grace swallowed hard. She'd left the beach house happy, thinking she'd found Mr. Right and believing all things good would happen for them. But Danny had left the beach house worried about the potential bad. It was no wonder neither of them had seen the other's perspective. They were at two ends of a very broad spectrum.

"I'm sorry, too. I was so happy I didn't think things through. Had I known—"

Sarah pounded on her tray with a squeal. Grace grimaced. "I forgot to feed her."

Danny calmly rose. "I can get that."

Grace's first instinct was to tell him to sit back down.

Their discussion wasn't really over. But wasn't it? What else was there to say? He was sorry. She was sorry. But they couldn't change the past. She didn't want a relationship. He'd hurt her and she rightfully didn't trust him. And he didn't want a relationship. Otherwise he wouldn't have promised not to kiss her again. There was nothing more to say. The discussion really was over.

"Do you remember how to make cereal?" Grace asked.

"The stuff in the box with a little milk, right?"

She nodded.

"I can handle it."

He strode into the kitchen and Grace took several long, steadying breaths.

His child had died.

She had always believed that nothing he could say would excuse the way he treated her when she told him she was pregnant.

But this did.

It didn't mean she would trust her heart to him, but it did mean she could forgive him.

That night Grace had dinner nearly prepared when Danny arrived. She directed him upstairs to change while she fed Sarah some baby food and by the time Sarah had eaten, Danny returned wearing jeans and a T-shirt. He looked as relaxed as he had their night at the beach house. Confession, apparently, had done him a world of good.

Incredibly nervous, Grace fussed over the salads.

Now that she knew about Danny's son everything was different. She almost didn't know how to treat him. His admissions had opened the door to their being friends, and being friendly would work the best for Sarah's sake. But could two people with their chemistry really be friends?

While Grace brought their salads to the table, Danny took his seat.

"You know, we never have gotten around to discussing a lot of things about Sarah."

Glad for the neutral topic, Grace said, "Like what?"

"For one, child support."

"Since we'll each have Sarah two weeks a month, I don't think either one of us should be entitled to child support. So don't even think of filing for any."

He laughed. "Very funny."

A tingle of accomplishment raced through her at his laughter, but she didn't show any outward sign of her pleasure. Instead she shrugged casually. "Hey, I make a decent salary. How do I know it wasn't your intention to file?"

"You never did tell me where you got a job."

"I work for a small accounting firm. Johnson and O'Hara."

"So you do okay financially?"

"Yeah." Grace smiled. "Actually they pay me double what your firm did."

He chuckled. "You got lucky."

"Yes, I did."

He glanced into the kitchen, then behind himself at

the living room. "And you seem to know how to use your money wisely."

"I bought this house the day I got my first job."

"The night I was grilling, I remembered you told me about remodeling your house while we ate that Sunday night at the beach house." He smiled across the table at her, and Grace's stomach flip-flopped. Lord, he was handsome. And nice. And considerate. And smart. And now she knew he wasn't mean-spirited or selfish, but wounded. Life had hurt him and he needed somebody like her to make him laugh.

Oh God, she was in trouble!

"You did a good job on the remodel."

"My cousin did most of it." Shifting lettuce on her dish, Grace avoided looking at him. "I was the grunt. He would put something in place, tack it with a nail or two then give me the nail gun to finish."

"It looks great." He took another bite of salad.

But Grace was too nervous to eat. She couldn't hate him anymore. But she couldn't really like him, either.

Or could she?

By telling her about his son, he'd both explained his behavior and proved he trusted her.

But he'd also said she didn't need to worry about him kissing her anymore.

Of course, he might have said that because she'd pushed him away the night before, reminding him that kissing only got them in trouble.

They finished their salads and Grace brought the roast beef, mashed potatoes and peas to the table. Unhappy with being ignored, Sarah pounded her teething ring on her high chair tray and screeched noisily.

"What's the matter, Sarah Bear," Grace crooned, as she poured gravy onto her mashed potatoes. Sarah screeched again and Grace laughed. "Oh, you want to sit on somebody's lap? Well, you can't."

She glanced at Danny. "Unless your daddy wants to hold you?"

Danny said, "Sure, I'll—"

But Grace stopped him. "No. You can't hold a baby in front of a plate with gravy on it. You would be wearing the gravy in about twenty seconds."

"If you want to eat your dinner in peace, I could take her into the living room, then eat when you're done."

He was so darned eager to please that Grace stared at him, drawing conclusions that made her heart tremble with hope. There was only one reason a man wanted to please a woman. He liked her. Which meant maybe Danny had only promised not to kiss her again because she'd stopped him, not because he didn't want to kiss her anymore.

Or she could be drawing conclusions that had absolutely no basis in fact.

"I'm fine. I like having Sarah at the table. When I said you might want to hold her I was just teasing her."

"Oh, okay."

Determined to keep her perspective and keep things light and friendly, Grace turned to the high chair. "So, Miss Sarah, you stay where you are."

"What's that thing your mother's got you wearing?"

Danny asked, pointing at the fuzzy swatch of material in the shape of a stuffed bear that had been sewn onto Sarah's shirt.

"It's a bear shirt."

Danny's fork stopped halfway to his mouth and he gave Grace a confused look. "What?"

"A bear shirt." Grace laughed. "From the day she was born, my dad called her Sarah Boo Beara…then Sarah Bear. Because the name sort of took, my parents buy her all kinds of bear things." She angled her fork at the bear on Sarah's shirt. "Push it."

"Push it?"

"The bear. Push it and see what happens."

Danny reached over and pushed the bear on Sarah's shirt. It squeaked. Sarah grinned toothlessly.

Danny jumped as if somebody had bitten him. "Very funny."

"It makes Sarah laugh and some days that's not merely a good thing. It's a necessity."

"I remember."

Of course, he remembered. He'd had a son. Undoubtedly lots of things he did for Sarah or things Sarah did would bring back memories for him. If he needed anything from Grace it might not be a relationship as much as a friend to listen to him. Just listen.

"Would you like to talk about it?"

Danny shook his head. "Not really."

Okay. She'd read that wrong. She took a quiet breath, realizing she'd been off base about him a lot, and maybe the smart thing here would be to stop trying to guess what he thought and only believe what he said. Including that he wouldn't be kissing her anymore. So she should stop romanticizing.

"If you ever do want to talk, I'm here."

"I know." He toyed with his fork then he glanced over at her with a wistful smile. "I sort of wonder what might have happened between us if I'd told you everything the morning after we'd slept together, as I had intended to."

Her heart thudded to a stop. "You were going to tell me?"

He nodded. "Instead the only thing I managed to get out was that I had to go away for a week." He paused, glancing down at the half-eaten food on his plate. "I really shouldn't have slept with you that night. I was still raw, but fighting it, telling myself it was time to move on. And I made a mistake."

"You don't get sole blame for that. I was the one who went down to the bar."

"Yeah, but I was the one who knew I wasn't entirely healed from my son's death and my divorce. The whole disaster was my fault."

"It takes two—"

"Grace, stop. Please."

His tone brooked no argument—as if she'd been pushing him to talk, when she hadn't—and Grace bristled. Though he'd said he didn't want to talk about this, he'd been the one to dip their toes into the conversation. Still, because it was his trouble, his life, they were discussing, he also had to be the one with the right to end it. "Okay."

He blew his breath out on a long sigh. "I'm not trying to hide things or run from things, but I just plain don't want to remember anymore. I'm tired of the past and don't like to remember it, let alone talk about it. I like living in the present."

"I can understand that."

"Good." He set his fork on his dish. "So do you want help with the dishes?"

She almost automatically said no, but stopped herself. Giving him something to do made life easier for both of them. "Sure."

He rose, gathering the plates. She lifted the meat platter and walked it to the refrigerator. The oppressive tension of the silence between them pressed on her chest. If the quiet was difficult for her, she couldn't even imagine how hard it was on Danny. Knowing he didn't want to think, to remember, she plunged them into the solace of chitchat.

"So what did you do at work today?"

Danny turned on the faucet to rinse their dishes. "The same old stuff. What did you do?"

"I'm in the process of reviewing the books for a company that wants to incorporate."

That caught his interest. "Oh, an IPO."

Grace winced at the excitement in his voice. "No, a small family business. The corporation will be privately held. The principals are basically doling out shares of stock to the family members who made the company successful, as a way to ensure ownership as well as appropriate distribution of profits."

"Ah."

"Not nearly as exciting as investing the fortunes of famous athletes, but it's good work. Interesting."

"Have you begun to do any investing for yourself?"

His question triggered an unexpected memory of telling him she'd gone to work for his investment firm because she wanted to learn about investing to be rich. The heat of embarrassment began to crawl up her neck. She'd meant what she said, but given everything that had happened between them, her enthusiastic pronouncement had probably fed the fire of his suspicions about her.

They'd really made a mess of things that night.

She walked back to the dining room table and retrieved the mashed potato bowl. "I'm working on getting the house paid off. So I haven't had a lot of spare cash."

"Since we'll be splitting expenses for Sarah, you should have some extra money then, right?"

She shrugged. "Maybe."

"Grace, I want to pay my fair share. And I can be pretty stubborn. So no maybes or probablys or whatevers. Let's really be honest about the money."

"Okay."

He stacked the dishes in the dishwasher. "Okay. So once we get everything straightened out I would like to open an account for you at Carson Services."

Grace laughed. "Right. Danny, even if I have spare cash from our sharing expenses for Sarah, I'm not sure I'll have more than a hundred dollars a month or so."

"A hundred dollars a month is good."

"Oh, really? You're going to open an investment account with a hundred dollars?"

He winced. "I thought I'd open it with a few thousand dollars of my own money. You know, to make up for what you've spent to date and you could add to it."

Grace sighed. "You told me to stop talking about the past and I did. So now I'm going to tell you to stop fretting about the money."

"But I—"

"Just stop. I don't want your money. I never did. When I said I wanted to be rich that night at the beach house, I was actually saying that I wanted my parents and me to be comfortable." She motioned around her downstairs. "Like this. This is enough. I am happy. I do not want your money. Can you accept that?"

He held her gaze for several seconds. Grace didn't even flinch, so that he would see from her expression that this was as important to her as no longer discussing the past was for him.

"Yes, I accept that."

"Okay."

Sliding under the covers that night, Grace was still annoyed by their money discussion. Not because he wanted to pay his fair share, and not even because she had brought his suspicions about her on herself, but because that one memory opened the door to a hundred more.

She remembered what it felt like to be with him. He'd made her feel so special. Wonderful. Perfect.

Warmth immediately filled her. So did the sense that she'd had during their weekend together. That they fit. That they were right for each other. She had been so happy that weekend, but she also remembered that *he'd* been happy too.

Was she so wrong to think *she* brought out the nice guy in him? And was it so wrong to believe that there was a chance that the nice guy could come out and stay out forever? And was it so wrong to think that maybe— just maybe—if the nice guy stayed out forever they could fall in love for real? Not fall into bed because they were sexually attracted. But fall in love. For real. To genuinely care about each other.

She didn't know, and she couldn't even clearly analyze the situation because they'd slept together and that one wonderful memory clouded her judgment.

Plus she'd already decided she wouldn't be second-guessing him anymore. He'd said she didn't have to worry about him kissing her again.

He didn't want her. She had to remember that.

CHAPTER EIGHT

GRACE awakened to the scent of pancakes and the sound of Sarah slapping her chubby hands against the bars of her crib.

"I'm coming."

She groggily pulled herself out of bed and lifted Sarah into her arms. Rain softly pitter-pattered on the roof. The scent of blueberry pancakes wafted through the air. It would have been a perfect morning except Grace had tossed and turned so much the night before that she'd slept in.

Though she had said she didn't want to get accustomed to having Danny around, after dressing Sarah for the day, she padded downstairs and into the kitchen area.

"Hey."

Danny looked up from the newspaper he was reading at the kitchen counter. "Good morning."

"I'm sorry, but I slept in. Could you take her?"

"And feed her?"

Grace nodded.

"Sure. Come on, Sarah Bear."

Sarah easily went to Danny and Grace turned and walked back though the living room, but at the stairs she paused, watching Danny as he held Sarah with one arm and prepared her cereal with the other. Rain continued to tap against the roof, making the house cozy and warm. Breakfast was made. She would have privacy to dress. It all seemed so perfect that Grace had a moment of pure, unadulterated sadness, realizing that *this* was what sleeping together too soon had cost them.

She drew in a breath and ran upstairs. There was no point crying over spilled milk. No point wishing for what might have been. And no way she could jeopardize the comfort level they had by yearning for a romance. Particularly with a man who so desperately needed to do things at his own pace, in his own way.

She showered, dressed and returned downstairs. Sarah sat in her high chair and cooed when Grace approached. Danny rose from the dining room table and walked into the kitchen.

"I'll microwave your pancakes. Just to warm them up."

"Thanks."

"Want some coffee?"

"Yes, but I'll get it." She laughed. "I told you, I don't want to get too accustomed to having help."

He leaned against the counter and crossed his arms on his chest. "We could share the nanny I hire."

She held up her hands to stop him. "Don't tempt me."

"Why not? What else is she going to do during the weeks you have Sarah?"

"Take yoga."

He burst out laughing. "Come on, Grace, at least think about it."

She poured herself a cup of coffee, then grabbed the cream from the refrigerator. "The part of me that wants help is being overruled by the part of me that loves the one-on-one time with Sarah."

He nodded. "Okay. Makes sense."

She turned and smiled at him. "Thanks."

He returned her smile. "You're welcome."

For a few seconds, they stood smiling at each other, then Grace's smile faded and she quickly turned away. She really liked him, and that triggered more phero-mones than a thousand bulging biceps. They were better off when she had disliked him, before his explanation and apology. Now instead of disagreeing and keeping their distance they were becoming friends, getting close, and she was wishing for things she couldn't have.

"By the way, my lawyer called this morning."

Brought back to the present by a very timely re-minder, Grace faced him. "Oh, yeah?"

Danny winced. "Yeah. The guy's a nut. He called me while he was shaving. He actually woke me." The mi-crowave buzzer rang. Unfolding his arms, Danny pushed away from the counter. "He asked about the progress on our agreement. I told him that you had told me you contacted a lawyer, and that lawyer had told you it was okay to sign, so you signed it, right?"

The casual, cozy atmosphere of Grace's little house shifted. Tension seeped into the space between them with words left unsaid. He hadn't signed their agreement. She had. But he hadn't. And it worried his lawyer. Or maybe it worried *him* and he used the call from his lawyer as a cover?

She swallowed, calling herself crazy for being suspicious. Shared custody was *her* idea. "I signed it."

"Great. Give it to me and I'll sign it, then we'll be set. According to my lawyer, once we have that in place we won't even need a hearing." Plate of warm pancakes in his hand, he faced her. "We simply begin sharing custody."

His pancakes suddenly looked like a bribe, and Grace froze, unable to take them from his hand. Until she reminded herself that Danny had nothing to gain by being nice to her. If anything *she* benefited from any agreement that kept them out of court.

She forced a smile and took the plate from his hands. "Sounds good. It's upstairs. I'll get it."

He glanced at his watch, then grimaced. "I have an early meeting today so unless you want your pancakes to get cold again, how about if you get it for me tonight. Tomorrow's Saturday, but I can take it to work on Monday and sign it in front of my secretary who can witness it. Then we'll make copies."

Calling herself every sort of fool for being suspicious, Grace walked to the table. "That sounds good." Eager to make up for her few seconds of doubt, she added, "But it's on top of my dresser. You could get it."

He waved a hand in dismissal. "We'll handle it tomorrow."

Grace drove to work, feeling like an idiot for mistrusting him. But walking from the parking garage, she reminded herself that it wasn't out of line for her to be suspicious of him. She might be prone to a little too much second-guessing about him, but he hadn't really told her a lot about his life. And he stopped the discussion any time they began to edge beyond surface facts.

Plus, *they* had a past. An unusual, unhappy past. He mistrusted her. When she told him she was pregnant, he kicked her out of his office. After that, she never tried to contact him again because she hadn't trusted him. She only took the baby to him for Sarah's sake. She hadn't expected him to want visitation, let alone have a hand in raising their daughter. But he did. He wanted full custody and had agreed to shared custody. To get Grace to give him that, he had to prove himself. Everything they'd done had been a negotiation of a sort.

She shouldn't magically feel that things between them had been patched up.

Except that he'd trusted her enough to tell him about his son.

Didn't that count as at least a step toward mended fences?

Yes, it did. Yet even knowing that he had good reason to be off his game something bothered her. Something in her gut said that Danny was too eager about their agreement and accepting shared custody, and she had no idea why.

Grace couldn't come up with a solid answer, even though the question popped into her head a million times that day. She returned home that evening edgy and annoyed, tired of running this scenario through her brain. Shared custody and the agreement had been *her* idea. She'd already signed the agreement. Week about with Sarah was the fair thing to do in their circumstance. The man had offered her the use of his nanny. He'd told her about his son. Yet something still nagged at her.

It didn't help that Sarah was grouchy. After a quiet and somewhat strained dinner, Danny excused himself to go to his room to work on a project that needed to be completed on Monday morning. Grace tried to stack the dishes in the dishwasher with Sarah crying in her high chair, but her patience quickly ran out. She lifted the baby and carried her up to Danny's room.

"Can you watch her while I finish clearing the kitchen?"

Looking too big for the little corner desk Grace had in her spare room more for decorative purposes than actual use, Danny faced her. "Grace, I—"

"Please." Grace marched into the room. "I know you have to get this project done for Monday morning, but I had a miserable day and I just need a few minutes to clean up." She dropped Sarah onto his lap. "When the dishes are done, I'll take her again."

With that she walked out, closing Danny's bedroom door behind her, leaving nothing but silence in her wake.

Danny glanced down at the little girl on his lap. "One of us made her angry and since I've been up here and you were the one with her in the kitchen, I'm blaming you."

Sarah screeched at him.

"Right. You can argue all you want but the fact remains that I was up here and you were down there with her."

He rose from the little desk chair and walked to the door, intending to take the baby to the living room where he and Sarah could watch TV or maybe play on the floor. But even before his hand closed around the knob, he had second thoughts. Grace said she wanted to clean the kitchen, but maybe what she needed was some peace and quiet. He glanced around, unsure of what to do. The room wasn't tiny, but it wasn't a center of entertainment, either.

"Any suggestions for how we can amuse ourselves for the next hour or so?" he asked Sarah as he shifted her into his arms so that he could look down at her. She smiled up at him and his heart did a crazy flip-flop. From this angle he didn't see as much of Cory in her features as he saw Grace. Were he to guess, he would say Sarah's eyes would some day be the same shade of violet that Grace's were.

She rubbed her little fist across her nose, then her right eye, the sign babies used when they were sleepy. Danny instinctively kissed the top of her head.

She peeked up and grinned at him and this time Danny's heart expanded with love. Not only had Sarah grown accustomed to him, but also he was falling in love with her. He was falling in love with the baby, happy living in Grace's home and having feelings for Grace he didn't dare identify. He knew she deserved a better man than he was. He'd made a promise to himself not to hurt her and he intended to keep it.

He looked down at Sarah, who yawned. "On, no, Sarah! You can't fall asleep this early. You'll wake up before dawn, probably ready to play and tomorrow's Saturday, the only day your mom gets to sleep in—"

He stopped talking because inspiration struck him. The thing to do would be to get Sarah ready for bed. That way she wouldn't fall asleep for at least another half hour and who knew? Maybe a bath would revive her? Plus he might make a few brownie points with Grace by keeping them so busy she could relax.

Pleased with that idea, he held Sarah against his shoulder, quietly opened his bedroom door and looked down the hall. Grace was nowhere in sight, and he could still hear the sounds of pots and pans in her kitchen.

He sneaked across the little hall and into her room. Inside he was immediately enfolded in a warm, sheltered feeling, the sense a man got when he felt at home. He squeezed his eyes shut, telling himself not to get so attached to Grace and her things that he again did something they'd both regret. He took a breath, then another and then another, reminding himself of all the reasons being too cozy with her was wrong.

Sarah wiped her nose in his shirt and snuggled into his shoulder, bringing him back to reality.

"No. No," he said, manipulating her into a different position before she could get too comfortable. "You'll be able to go to sleep soon enough if you let your daddy get you ready for bed."

He searched around the room for her baby tub, but

realized it was probably in the bathroom. Remembering that preparation was a parent's best trick when caring for a baby, he decided to get everything ready before he brought his sopping wet baby from the bathroom. He laid a clean blanket on the changing table, then pulled open the top draw of a white chest of drawers that had bears painted on the knobs. Inside were undershirts and socks so tiny they looked about thumb-size. Knowing those were too small, he closed the drawer, and opened the next one, seeking pajamas. He found them, then located the stash of disposable diapers, and arranged them on the changing table.

With everything ready he took Sarah to the bathroom. Holding her with one arm, he filled the baby tub he'd placed inside the regular bathtub, found her soap and shampoo and the baby towel that hung on the rack.

That was when he realized she was fully dressed and he was still wearing his suit trousers. In an executive decision, he pronounced it too late to do anything about his trousers and laid her on the fluffy carpet in front of the tub to remove her clothes.

She giggled and cooed and he shook his head. "Let's just hope you're this happy after I put you in the water."

She grinned at him.

Returning her smile, he lifted her to eye level. "Ready?"

She laughed and patted his cheeks.

"Okay, then." He dipped her into the tub and when she didn't howl or stiffen up, he figured she was one of the babies who loved to sit in water. Grateful, he kept one hand at her back as he wet a washcloth and squeezed a few drops of liquid soap on it, amazed by how quickly baby care was coming back to him.

"So you like the water?" Danny said, entertaining Sarah with chitchat as he washed her, just in case any part of bathtime had the potential to freak her out. She merely gooed and cooed at him, even when he washed her hair. Pleased by his success, he rinsed off all the soapsuds, rolled her in the soft terry-cloth baby towel and carried her back to Grace's room.

Not in the slightest uncomfortable, Sarah chewed a blue rubber teething ring while Danny put on her diaper and slid her into pajamas.

When she was completely dressed, he took her out into the hallway. He heard the sounds of the television—indicating Grace was done filling the dishwasher and probably waiting for the cycle to be complete so she could put everything away—and turned to the stairs, but his conscience tweaked. He'd been here five days and he hadn't done anything more than make pancakes, help with dishes and grill a few things. This was the first time he'd really helped with the baby. It seemed totally wrong to take Sarah downstairs and disturb the only private moments he'd allowed Grace.

He turned and walked back into Grace's bedroom. "So what do we do?"

Sarah rubbed her eyes again.

Danny frowned. He didn't have a bottle for her, but she didn't seem hungry. Or fussy. All she appeared to be was sleepy. Now that they'd wasted almost an hour getting her ready for bed, it didn't seem too early to let her fall asleep. The only question was, could she fall asleep without a bottle?

He remembered a comment Grace had made about making up stories for Sarah, and walked to the bed. If he laid Sarah in her crib, he ran the risk that she'd cry and Grace's private time would be disturbed. It seemed smarter to sit on the bed and tell Sarah a story and see if she'd fall asleep naturally.

He sat. Sarah snuggled against his chest. But sitting on the edge of Grace's bed was incredibly uncomfortable, so he scooted back until he was leaning against the headboard.

"This is better."

Sarah blinked up at him sleepily.

"Okay. Let's see. You clearly like bears since your grandfather blended a bear into your name, so let's make up a story about a bear."

She blinked again. Heavier this time. He scooted down a little further, then decided he might as well lie down, too.

Two hours later, Grace awoke on the sofa. She'd fallen asleep! Danny was going to kill her.

She ran up the steps and to Danny's room, but it was empty. Panicked, she raced across the hall and without turning on the light saw his shadowy form on her bed. She tiptoed into the room and peered down to discover he was not only sleeping on her bed with Sarah, he'd also put the baby in her pajamas for the night.

Both the baby and her daddy slept deeply, comfortably. Little Sarah lay in the space between his chest and his arm, snuggled against him in a pose of trust. Danny looked naturally capable. Grace wished she had a camera.

Careful not to disturb Danny, she reached down and lifted Sarah from his arms. The baby sniffled and stretched, but Grace "Shhed," her back to sleep and laid her in her crib.

Then she turned to her bed, her heart in her throat. Danny looked so comfortable and so relaxed that she didn't want to disturb him. The peaceful repose of his face reminded her of the morning she'd awakened in his bed in the beach house, and she involuntarily sat down beside him.

Unable to help herself, she lovingly brushed a lock of hair from his forehead. She wasn't going to fall into her black pit of recriminations again about sleeping together. She already knew that had been a mistake. No need to continue berating herself. Life had handled their punishment for prematurely sleeping together by using it to keep them apart. What she wanted right now was just a couple of seconds, maybe a minute, to look at him, to be happy he was here, to enjoy the fact that he loved their daughter so she wouldn't have to worry when Sarah was in his care.

She scooted a little closer on the bed, remembered waking up that morning at the beach house, laughed softly at how glad she had been that she'd had the chance to sneak away and brush her teeth before he woke up, and then sighed as she recalled making love in the shower.

She remembered thinking that she'd never love

another man the way she loved Danny and realized it was still true. He had her heart and she wasn't even sure how he'd done it. Except that he was cute, and sweet, and nice, and she desperately wanted to fill the aching need that she could now see he had.

But he wouldn't let her.

And that was what was bothering her. That was why she grabbed onto her suspicions like a lifeline. As long as she mistrusted him, she could hold herself back. But now that he'd told her about his son, explaining his irrational behavior, she had forgiven him. And once she'd forgive him, she'd begun falling in love again.

But he didn't love her. He didn't want to love her. If she didn't stop her runaway feelings, she was going to get hurt again.

After another breath, she lightly shook his shoulder and whispered, "Danny?"

He grumbled something unintelligible and she smiled. Damn he was cute. It really didn't seem fair that she had to resist him.

"Danny, if you don't want to get up, I can sleep in your room, but you'll have to wake up with Sarah when she cries for her two o'clock feeding."

The threat of being responsible for Sarah must have penetrated, because he took a long breath, then groggily sat up.

"Want help getting across the hall?"

He stared at her, as if needing to focus, and reached for her hand, which was still on his shoulder. His fingers were warm and his touch gentle, sending reaction from

Grace's fingertips to her toes. She remembered how sweet his kisses had been. She remembered how giving, yet bold he was as a lover. She remembered how safe she'd felt with him, how loved.

In the silence of the dark night, their gazes stayed locked for what felt like forever, then he put his hands on her shoulders and ran them down her back, along the curve of her waist and up again.

Grace swallowed and closed her eyes, savoring the feeling that she remembered from that summer night. Not sexual attraction, but emotional connection, expressed through physical attraction. Whatever was between them was powerful, but it was also sweet. By caring for Sarah tonight he'd shown her what she'd instinctively understood about him. That deep down he was a good guy. He'd kept Sarah beyond the time he'd needed to for Grace to get her work done, dressed her in pajamas and fallen asleep with the baby in his arms.

He might dismiss it or downplay it, but he couldn't deny it and that meant they were at a crossroad. He liked her enough to do something kind for her. It might be too soon for him to fall in love again. Or he might not want to fall in love again. But he was falling. And she didn't have to tell him she was falling, too. He could surely see it in her eyes.

Gazing into his dark eyes, Grace held her breath, hoping, almost praying he was thinking the same thing she was and that he had the courage to act on it.

CHAPTER NINE

IN THE dark, quiet bedroom that radiated warmth and the comfort of home, Danny stared at Grace. All he wanted to do was crawl under the covers of her bed with her. Not to make love but to sleep. He was tired, but also he simply needed the succor of this night. The peaceful feeling a man got when his baby was tucked away in her crib, sleeping like an angel, and the mother of his baby was tucked under his arm. The desire was instinctive, nearly primal, and so natural he hadn't thought it. It had overtaken him. Almost as if it wasn't something he could stop or change.

But every time he'd given in to his instincts, he'd failed somebody. He'd failed Lydia, he'd failed Cory, and he'd even failed Grace by not believing her when she told him she was pregnant. Did he really want to fail her again?

No.

He backed away from the temptation of Grace, his hands sliding off her in a slow, sad way, savoring every second of her softness for as long as he could before it was gone.

He hadn't said anything foolish like how beautiful she was or how much he had missed her or how the instant closeness they had shared was coming back to him. He hadn't done anything he couldn't take back like kiss her. He could get out of this simply by saying goodnight and leaving the room.

"Good night."

She swallowed. "Good night."

And Danny walked out of the room.

Grace sat on the bed. It was still warm from where he lay. She could smell the subtle hint of his aftershave.

She dropped her head to her hands. If she'd needed any more reason to stay away from Danny, he'd given it to her tonight. She'd watched the play of emotions on his face display the battle going on in his brain as he'd stared at her, wanting her, yet denying himself. She could have been insulted or hurt; instead she saw just how strong he was. How determined he could be to deny himself what he wanted, even when it was probably clear to him that she wanted it, too.

And it was her loss. She knew it the whole way to her soul.

For the second time since he'd moved in with Grace, Danny awakened happy. The night before he'd spent time with Sarah and had very successfully cared for her, proving to himself that he didn't need to be afraid about the weeks he would spend with his daughter. He'd also successfully stepped away from temptation with Grace.

He wanted her, but he didn't want to hurt her. Some day she would thank him.

As he dressed, he heard the sounds of Sarah awakening and Grace walking down the stairs to get her a bottle. When he was sure she had returned to her room to dress and get the baby ready for the day, he rushed downstairs, strode into the kitchen and retrieved the ingredients for pancakes.

Twenty minutes later she came down the stairs and he turned from the stove. "Good morning."

Wearing jeans and a pale blue top that made her eyes seem iridescent, Grace carried the baby to her high chair.

"Good morning."

She was beautiful in an unassuming, yet naturally feminine way that always caused everything male in Danny to sit up and take notice. But he didn't mind that. In fact, now that he knew he could control the emotional side of their relationship, he actually liked noticing Grace. What man didn't want to appreciate a beautiful woman?

As she puttered, getting the baby settled in the high chair with a teething ring, Danny looked his fill at the way her T-shirt hugged her full breasts and her blue jeans caressed her bottom. But what really drew him was her face. Her violet eyes sparkled with laughter and her full lips lifted in a smile. If his walking away the night before had affected her, she didn't show it. She was one of the most accepting, accommodating people he'd ever met.

He took a stack of pancakes to the table and she sniffed the air. "Blueberry again."

He winced. "They're my only specialty."

She surprised him by laughing. "You say that as if you'd like to learn to cook."

His reaction to that was so unexpected that he stopped halfway to the kitchen and he faced her again. "I think I do."

She took her seat at the table. "I don't know why that seems so novel to you. Lots of men cook."

But Danny didn't want to cook. He wanted to please Grace. Not in a ridiculous, out-of-control way, but in a way that fulfilled his part of the responsibility. Still, with only a week left in their deal to live together it was too late now to find a class.

Grace plopped a pancake on her plate as Sarah pounded her high chair tray. "You could get a cookbook."

Now that idea had merit.

"Or I could teach you."

And that idea had even more merit. He would get the knowledge he needed to do his part, and he'd have a perfect opportunity to spend time with Grace. Normal time. Not fighting a middle-of-the-night attraction. Not wishing for things he couldn't have. But time to get even more adjusted to having her in his world without giving in to every whim, sexual craving or desire for her softness.

"I'd like that."

She smiled at him. "Great. This morning we'll go shopping for groceries."

Reaching into the cupboard for syrup, he said, "Shopping?"

"Shopping is the first step in cooking. You can't

make what you don't have. If you'd tried to prepare these pancakes tomorrow," she said, pointing at her dish, "you would have been sadly disappointed because the blueberries would have been gone. That's why we're going shopping today."

He didn't really want to go to a store, but she had a point. Unfortunately her suggestion also had a fatal flaw. "How am I going to know what to buy if I don't yet know how to cook anything?"

"I'm going to help you."

"Right."

Sarah screeched her displeasure at being left out of the conversation. Danny took his seat at the table and before Grace could turn to settle the baby, he broke off a small bite of pancake and set it in her open mouth.

She grinned at him.

And Danny felt his world slide into place. What he felt was beyond happiness. It was something more like purpose or place. That was it. He had a place. He had a child, and a friend in his child's mother. In a sense, Grace getting pregnant had given him back his life. As long as he didn't try to make this relationship any more than it was, he had a family of sorts.

In the grocery store, Grace had serious second thoughts about her idea of teaching Danny to cook. He wanted to learn to steam shrimp and prepare crème brûlée. Her expertise ran more along the lines of pizza rolls and brownies. And the brownies weren't even scratch brownies. They were from a boxed mix.

"How about prime rib?"

"I'm not exactly sure how that's made, either."

"We need a cookbook."

"Or we could start with less complex things like grilled steak and baked potatoes."

Standing by the spice counter, he slowly turned to face her, a smile spreading across his mouth. "You don't know how to cook, either."

"That's a matter of opinion. I know the main staples. I can bake a roast that melts in your mouth, fix just about any kind of potato you want and steam vegetables. My lasagna wins raves at reunions—"

"Reunions?"

"You know. Family reunions. Picnics. Where all the aunts and uncles and cousins get together and everybody brings his or her specialty dish, plays volleyball or softball, coos over each other's kids and the next morning wakes up with sore muscles because most of us only play sports that one day every year."

He laughed.

"You've never been to a family reunion?"

"I don't have much of a family. My dad was an only child, and though my mother had two siblings, her brother became a priest and her sister chose not to have kids."

She gaped at him. "You're kidding."

"Why are you so surprised. *Your* parents had only one child."

"My parents had one child because my dad was disabled in an automobile accident. He appears fine and he can do most things, but he never could go back to work. It's why my parents have so little money. We had to live on what my mother could make."

"Oh."

Seeing that he was processing that, Grace stepped over to the spices and pulled out a container of basil. She had to wonder if the reason Danny couldn't seem to love wasn't just the mistake of his marriage, but a result of his entire past. Could a person who'd only seen one marriage, then failed at his own, really believe in love?

"I can also make soup."

"What kind?"

"Vegetable and chicken and dumpling."

"Ah. A gourmet."

"Now, don't get snooty. I think you're really going to like the chicken and dumpling. I have to use a spaetzle maker."

"What the hell is a spaetzle maker?"

His confusion about a cooking utensil only served to confirm Grace's theory that Danny couldn't love because he knew so little about the simple, ordinary things other people took for granted. "It's a fancy word for a kitchen gadget that makes very small dumplings."

"Why don't you just call it that?"

"Because I'm not the one who decided what it's called. It's German or something. Besides, spaetzle maker sounds more official."

"Right."

Grace laughed. She was having fun. Lots of fun. The kind of fun they probably would have had if she and Danny had let their relationship develop slowly. They were so different that they'd desperately needed time to get to know each other, to become familiar with each other's worlds, and to integrate what worked and get rid of what didn't. From Danny's eagerness to learn and his curiosity, it was clear something was missing in his world. And from the way he reacted to the simplicity of her life it was obvious she wouldn't have been able to stay the same if they'd actually had a relationship. That was also why Sarah needed both of them. Neither one of them was *wrong* in the way they lived. It was all a matter of choices.

They spent over double what Grace normally allotted for food, but Danny paid the bill. When she tried to give him her share, he refused it, reminding her that she'd paid for the first week's groceries. Another proof that Danny was innately fair. A good man. Not the horrible man who tossed her out of his office when she told him she was pregnant. But a man trying to get his bearings after the loss of a child.

At two o'clock that afternoon, with Sarah napping and Danny standing about three inches behind her, Grace got out her soup pot.

"Could you watch from a few feet back?"

"I'm curious."

"Well, be curious over by the counter." He stepped away from her and to keep the conversation flowing so he didn't pout, Grace said, "Soup is good on a chilly fall day like this."

Danny leaned against the counter and crossed his arms on his chest. "I think you're showing off."

"Showing off?"

"I doubted your abilities, so you're about to dazzle me with your spaetzle maker."

She laughed. "The spaetzle maker doesn't come into play for a while yet. Plus, there's very little expertise to soup," she said, dropping the big pot on the burner. "First you get a pot."

He rolled his eyes.

"Then you fill it halfway with water." She filled a large bowl with water and dumped the water into the big pot on the stove. "You add an onion, one potato, a stalk of celery and a chicken."

He gaped at her. "You're putting that entire chicken into the pot?"

"Yes."

Now he looked horrified.

She laughed. "Come on. This is how my grandmother did it." While he stood gaping at her, looking afraid to comment, she reached for the chicken bouillon cubes.

His eyes widened. "You're cheating!"

"Not really. The only thing bouillion cubes accomplishes is to cut down on cooking time."

"It's still cheating."

"I'm starting to notice a trend here. You're against anything that saves time."

"I want to learn to cook correctly."

She shrugged. "I need to be able to save time." With everything in the pot, she washed her hands then dried them with a paper towel.

"Now what?"

"Now, I'm going to take advantage of the fact that Sarah's still napping and read."

"Really?"

"Even with the bouillion cubes, the soup needs to cook at least an hour. It's best if we give it two hours." She glanced at the clock on the stove. "So until Sarah wakes I'm going to read."

"What should I do?"

"Weren't you working on something last night?"

He pouted. "Yeah, but I can't go any further because I left an important file at my office."

She sighed. "So I have to entertain you?"

He actually thought about that. For a few seconds Grace was sure the strong man in him would say no. Instead he laughed and said, "Yes. Somebody's got to entertain me."

Grace only stared at him. The night before she would have sworn he was firmly against getting involved with her, but today he was happy to be in her company. It didn't make sense—

Actually it did. The night before they were both considering sleeping together. Today they were making soup. Laughing. Happy. Not facing a life choice. Just having fun in each other's company. No stress. No worries. And wasn't that her real goal? To make him comfortable enough that Sarah's stays with him would be pleasant?

That was exactly her goal. So she couldn't waste such a wonderful opportunity.

"Do you know anything about gardening?"

"No."

"Ever played UNO?"

He gave her a puzzled look. "What's an Uno?"

"Wow, either you've led dull life or I've been overly entertained." Deciding she'd been overly entertained by a dad who couldn't do much in the way of physical things, Grace had a sudden inspiration. "If your mother's an expert at rummy, I know you've played that."

He glanced down at his fingernails as if studying them. "A bit."

"Oh, you think you're pretty good, don't you?"

"I'm a slouch."

"Don't sucker me!"

"Would I sucker you?"

"To get me to let my guard down so you could beat me, yes." She paused, then headed to the dining room buffet and the cards. "If you think you have to sucker me, you must not be very good."

"I'm exceptional."

She grinned. "I knew it."

Just then, a whimper floated from the baby monitor on the counter.

Grace set the cards back in the drawer. "So much for rummy. I'll try to get her back to sleep but I'm betting she wants to come downstairs."

"Why did she wake up so soon?"

"She probably heard us talking. That's why she didn't roll over and go back to sleep. She wants to be in on the action."

"Great. We'll play rummy with her in the high chair."

She paused on her way to the steps. "We could, but wouldn't it be more fun to spend a few minutes with Sarah first?"

He nodded. "Yeah. You're right."

As Grace went up the steps Danny took a long breath. He, Grace and the baby had had a good time shopping. He and Grace had had fun putting away the groceries and getting the soup into the pot. Now they would spend even more time together, and no doubt it would be fun.

He rubbed his hand across the back of his neck. The whole morning had been so easy—so right—that he knew he was correct in thinking that a friendship between him and Grace gave him the family, the connection, he so desperately wanted. But he also knew he was getting too close to a line he shouldn't cross—unless he wanted to fall in love with her and make their family a real family. He didn't want to hurt her, but right now, in his gut, he had an optimistic sense that he wouldn't. And the night before he'd seen in her eyes that she wanted what he wanted. For them to fall in love. She didn't have to say the words for Danny to know that she trusted him. She believed in him. He'd hurt her once, yet she trusted that he wouldn't hurt her again.

She believed in him and maybe the trick to their situation wouldn't be to take this one step at a time, but to trust what Grace saw in him, rather than what he knew about himself.

He walked into the kitchen and lifted the lid from the

pot. He sniffed the steam that floated out and his mouth watered. Even if soup was simple fare and even though he absolutely believed Grace had cheated with the bouillion cube, it smelled heavenly. He'd trusted her about spending two weeks here with her and Sarah, and had acclimated to being in a family again, albeit a nontraditional one. He'd trusted Grace about the soup, and it appeared he would be getting a tasty dinner. He'd trusted her about relaxing with Sarah and he now had a relationship with his daughter.

Could he trust her instinct that he wouldn't hurt her? Or let her down the way he'd let Lydia down?

Grace came down the steps carrying smiling Sarah.

When the baby immediately zeroed in on him, he said, "Hey, kid."

She yelped and clapped her hands.

"She does a lot of screeching and yelping. We've got to teach her a few words."

"Eventually. Right now, I think playing with the blocks or maybe the cone and rings are a better use of our time."

Danny was about to ask what the cone and rings were, but he suddenly had a very vivid memory of them. He saw Cory on the floor, brightly colored rings in a semicircle in front of him. He remembered teaching Cory to pick up the rings in order of size and slide them onto the cone.

And the memory didn't hurt. In fact, it made him smile. Cory had always had an eye for color. Maybe Sarah did, too? Or maybe Danny didn't care how smart

Sarah was or where her gifts were? Maybe his being so concerned about Cory's gifts was part of what had pushed Lydia away from him?

Forcing himself into the present, Danny glanced around. "Where's the toy box?"

"I don't have one. Sarah's toys are in the bottom drawer of the buffet in the dining area."

He walked over to it. "Curse of a small house?"

"Yes. This is the other reason I hesitated to talk with you about opening an investment account for me. I definitely need something with more space and I'm considering buying another house, and if I have extra money that's probably where it will go."

He opened the bottom drawer, found the colorful cone and rings and pulled it out. Returning to the area that served as a living room, he handed Grace the cone and sat on the sofa.

As Grace dumped the multicolored rings on the floor in front of Sarah, Danny cautiously said, "You know, we've never made a firm decision about child support."

She glanced up at him with a smile. "Yes, we did. I told you I wouldn't pay you any."

Her comment made him laugh and suddenly Danny felt too far away. He slid off the sofa and positioned himself on the floor across from Grace with Sarah between them, using the baby as a buffer between him and the woman who—whether she knew it or not—was tempting him to try something he swore he'd never try again. Even the idea of *trying* was new. He was shaky at best about trusting himself, and Sarah's happiness also tied into their situation. He couldn't act hastily, or let his hormones have control.

"Actually I think if we went to court a judge would order me to pay you something. So, come on. Let's really talk about this."

Grace busied herself making sure all the rings were within Sarah's reach. "Okay, if you want to pay something every month, why don't you put a couple hundred dollars a month into a college fund for Sarah?"

"Because she doesn't need a college fund. I can afford to pay for schooling." He took a breath, remembering that the last time they'd broached this subject she'd made him stop—the same way he made her stop when they got too far into his past. But resolving child support for their daughter was different than rehashing a past he desperately needed to forget. They had to come to an agreement on support.

"Look, I know you don't want to talk about this. But we have to. I don't feel right not contributing to her day-to-day expenses."

"I already told you that we're going to be sharing custody," Grace said as she gently guided Sarah's hand to take the ring she was shoving into her mouth and loop it onto the cone. "I will have her one week, but you will have her the next. Technically that's the way we'll share her expenses."

"I'd still like to—"

"Danny, I have a job. My house is nearly paid off. When I sell it, the money I get will be my down payment for the new one. I have a plan. It works. We're fine."

"I know. I just—"

Though Danny had thought she was getting angry, she playfully slapped his knee. "Just for one afternoon will you please relax?"

He peered at her hand, then caught her gaze. "You slapped me."

She grinned. "A friendly tap to wake you up, so you'll finally catch on that I'm right."

This was what he liked about her. She didn't have to win every argument. She also knew when to pull back. *Before* either one of them said something they'd regret, rather than after. It was a skill or sixth sense he and Lydia had never acquired. Plus, she had wonderfully creative ways of stepping away and getting him to step away. Rather than slammed doors and cold shoulders, she teased him. And she let him tease her.

"Oh, yeah? So what you're saying is that friendly tapping between us is allowed?"

"Sure. Sometimes something physical is the only way to get someone's attention."

"You mean like this?" He leaped behind Sarah, caught Grace around the shoulders, and nudged her to the floor in one fluid movement, so he could tickle her.

"Hey!" she yelped, trying to get away from him when he tickled her ribs. "You *had* my attention."

"I had your attention, but you weren't getting my point, so I'm making sure you see how serious I am when I say you should take my money."

She wiggled away from him. "I don't need your money."

"I can see that," he said, catching her waist and dragging her back. "But I want to give it."

He tickled her again and she cried, "Uncle! I give up! Give me a thousand dollars and we'll call it even."

"I gave you more than that for helping with Orlando," he said, catching her gaze. When their eyes met, his breathing stopped. Reminded of the bonus and Orlando, vivid images of their weekend came to Danny. He stopped tickling. She stopped laughing. His throat worked.

In the year that had passed he'd all but forgotten she existed, convinced that she had lied about her pregnancy and left his employ because she was embarrassed that her scheme had been exposed. Now he knew she'd been sick, dependent upon the bonus that he'd given her for expenses and dependent upon her parents for emotional support that *he* should have given her.

"I'm so sorry about everything."

She whispered, "I know."

"I would give anything to make it up for the hurt I caused you."

"There's no need."

He remembered again how she had been that weekend. Happy, but also gracious. She wouldn't take a promotion she hadn't deserved. She wouldn't pry, was kind to Orlando, never overstepped her boundaries. And he'd hurt her. Chances were, he'd hurt her again.

Still, he wanted so much to kiss her that his chest ached and he couldn't seem to overrule the instinct that was as much emotional as it was physical. He liked her.

He just plain liked her. He liked being with her, being part of her life, having her in his life.

He lowered his head and touched his lips to hers, telling himself that if he slid them into a simple, uncomplicated romance with no expectation of grandeur, she wouldn't be hurt. He wouldn't be hurt. Both would get what they wanted.

His mouth slid across hers slowly at first, savoring every second of the physical connection that was a manifestation of the depth of his feelings for her. She answered, equally slowly, as if as hesitant as he was, but also as unable to resist the temptation. When the slight meeting of mouths wasn't enough her lips blossomed to life under his, meeting him, matching him, then oh so slowly opening.

It was all the invitation Danny needed. He deepened the kiss, awash with the pleasure of being close to someone as wonderful as Grace. Happiness virtually sang through his veins. Need thrummed through him. For the first time since she'd brought Sarah to him, his thoughts didn't automatically tumble back to their beach house weekend. They stayed in the present, on the moment, on the woman in his arms and the desire to make love. To touch her, to taste her, to cherish every wonderful second. To build a future.

But the second the future came into play, Danny knew he was only deluding himself. He'd tried this once and failed. He'd lost a child, broken his wife. Spent a year mourning his loss alone in the big house so hollow and empty it echoed around him. He knew the reality of loss. How it destroyed a person. Emptied a life. He couldn't go through it again, but more than that, he wouldn't force Grace to.

CHAPTER TEN

DANNY broke the kiss, quickly rose from the floor and extended his hand to Grace. When she was on her feet, he spun away and Grace's stomach knotted.

"Danny?"

He rubbed both hands down his face. "Grace, this is wrong."

"No, it isn't." Glad for the opportunity to finally discuss their feelings instead of guessing, she walked over and grabbed him by the upper arm, turning him to face her. "This is us. We like each other. Naturally. We're like toast and butter or salt and pepper. We fit."

He laughed harshly. "Fit? Are you sure you want to say you fit with me?"

She didn't hesitate. "Yes."

He shook his head. "Grace, please. Please, don't. Don't fit with me. Don't even *want* to fit with me. If you were smart you wouldn't even want to be my friend."

At that her chin came up. If he was going to turn her away again, to deny her his love, or even the chance to be part of his life, this time she would make him explain. "Why?"

"Because I'm not good for you. I'm not good for anybody."

"Why?"

He raked his fingers through his short black hair. "Stop!"

"No. You say you're not good for me. I say you are. And I will not stop pursuing you."

"Then I'll leave."

"Great. Run. If that's your answer to everything, then you run."

He groaned and walked away as if annoyed that she wouldn't let him alone. "I'm not running. I'm saving you."

"I don't think you are. I also don't think you're a coward who runs. So just tell me what's wrong!"

He pivoted to face her so quickly that Grace flinched. "Tell you? Tell you what? That I failed at my marriage and hurt the woman I adored? Tell you that I don't want to do it again?"

His obsidian eyes were bright with pain. His voice seemed to echo from a dark, sacred place. A place of scars and black memories and wounds. A place he rarely visited and never took another person. Still, broken marriages were common. And though she understood his had hurt him, she also suspected even *he* knew it was time to get beyond his.

Her heart breaking for him, Grace whispered, "How do you know that you'll fail?"

Stiff with resistance, he angrily countered, "How do you know that I won't?"

"Because you're good. You may not know it but I see it every day in how you treat me and how you treat Sarah."

"Grace, you are wrong. I use people. Just ask my ex-wife. She'll tell you I'm a workaholic. If you called her right now, she'd probably even accurately guess that I'm only here because I need to raise my daughter because I need an heir. Carson Services needs an heir."

"Well, she'd be wrong. If you only wanted to raise Sarah because Carson Services needs an heir you could take me to court."

"Unless I didn't want you digging into my past."

That stopped her.

"What if this is all about me not wanting you to take me to court?" he asked, stepping close. "What if there is something so bad in my past that I know even you couldn't forgive it?"

She swallowed. Possibilities overwhelmed her. Not only did having a hidden sin in his past explain why he agreed to live with her and their daughter when letting his lawyers handle their situation would have been much easier, but it also explained why he always stepped back, always denied himself and her.

Still, she couldn't imagine what he could have done. He wasn't gentle and retiring by any means. But he also wasn't cruel or vindictive. He wasn't the kind to take risks or live on the edge. She might have told herself to stop guessing, to quit ascribing characteristics to him he didn't deserve, but she'd also lived with him for a week. Almost fifteen hours a day. She'd seen him *choose* to make breakfast, *choose* to bathe Sarah, *choose* to give Grace breaks. She didn't believe he could be cruel or do something so horrible it couldn't be forgiven.

She took a breath, then another. "I don't think there is something in your past that can't be forgiven."

"What if I told you that I killed my son?"

Her heart in her throat, more aware of the pain that would cause him than any sort of ramification it would have on their relationship, she said, "You couldn't have killed your son."

"It was an accident, but the accident was my fault."

Grace squeezed her eyes shut. An accident that was his fault. Of course. That accounted for so many things in his life and how he had treated her that before this hadn't added up.

But accidents were circumstances that somehow got out of someone's control. He hadn't deliberately killed his child. He couldn't deliberately kill his child. That was why he was so tortured now.

"Danny, it wasn't your fault."

His eyes blazed. "Don't you forgive me! And don't brush it off as if my son's life was of no consequence. I was in charge of him that morning. *I* knew he was in the mood to push me. He wanted to remove the training wheels from his bike and I refused, but he kept arguing, begging, pleading. When my cell phone rang, I should have ignored it. But my natural reaction kicked in, I grabbed it, answered it and gave him the chance to prove to me how good he was on his bike by darting out into the street right into the path of an SUV."

He paused, raked his fingers through his hair again and his voice dropped to a feather-light whisper. "A neighbor hit him. She doesn't come out of her house now. I ruined a lot of lives that morning."

The tick of the clock was the only sound in the room. Grace stood frozen, steeped in his pain, hurting for him.

"Not quite as sure of me now, are you?"

She swallowed. "It wasn't your fault."

He ran his hands down his face. "It was my fault. And I live with it every day. And I miss my son and I remember the look on my wife's face." Seeming to be getting his bearings, he blew his breath out on a long gust and faced her. "And I won't do that to you."

He headed for the stairway. Panicked, knowing they were only at the tip of this discussion, Grace said, "What if I—"

He stopped at the bottom of the steps. His face bore the hard, cold expression she remembered from the day she told him she was pregnant.

"You don't get a choice. You don't get a say. This pain is mine."

He ran up the steps and Grace collapsed on her sofa. Bending forward, she lifted Sarah from the floor and squeezed her to her chest, suddenly understanding why he didn't want her digging into his past. It could give her plenty of grounds to keep him from getting custody—even shared. But it also gave her a foot in the door to keep the baby away from him completely.

And she hated to admit she was considering it. Not because of what had happened with his son, but because he couldn't seem to get beyond it. What did it mean for Sarah that her father wouldn't let himself love again?

She took a breath, knowing her fears were premature because they had another week to live together, another week for him to recognize that though he didn't want to forget his son, he also had a daughter who needed him. She shouldn't jump to conclusions.

But twenty minutes later he came downstairs, suitcases in hand.

"We have another week to live together."

"Grace, I'm done." He shrugged into his jacket. "Besides, I never signed the agreement. This was a mistake anyway."

With that he opened the door, and stepped out, but he turned one final time and looked at Sarah, then his gaze slowly rose to catch Grace's. She saw the regret, the pain, the need. Then she watched him quickly erase it as determination filled his dark eyes. He stepped out into the September afternoon, closing the door behind him with a soft click.

Danny walked into the empty foyer of his huge house and listened to the echo his suitcase made as he set it on the floor, knowing this was the rest of his life, and for the first time totally, honestly, unemotionally committed to accepting it. He wouldn't risk hurting Grace. Telling his story that afternoon, he remembered in vivid detail how unworthy he was to drag another person into his life. Now that Grace knew his mistake, he didn't expect to even get visitation with Sarah. He expected to live his life alone, the perfect candidate to serve Carson Services and pass on the family legacy.

To Sarah. A little girl who wouldn't know him, probably wouldn't know about Carson Services, but who shared his bloodline. When she came of age, Danny would offer her the chance to train to take over the family business, but would Grace let her? No mother would sentence her daughter to even a few hours a week with a cold, distant father.

Walking up the ornate curved stairway of the huge home that went to the next Carson, Danny had to wonder if that wasn't a good thing.

CHAPTER ELEVEN

A MONTH later, seated at the slim wooden table in the hearing room in the courthouse, Danny wasn't entirely sure why he had come to this proceeding. Grace's reasons for being here were a no-brainer. She'd had her lawyer set the hearing to make her case for Danny not getting custody. She could probably get enough reasons on the record to preclude him from even *seeing* their baby again.

But he knew she wouldn't do that. After his confession to her, and a week of wallowing in misery in his lonely house, he'd pulled himself up by his bootstraps and gone back to work like the sharp CEO he was, and his life had fallen into a strong, comfortable routine. Once he'd gotten his bearings and stopped feeling sorry for himself, he'd recognized that *all* was not lost. Grace wouldn't keep Sarah from him. She would be kind enough—or maybe fair enough to Sarah—to let him have visitation, even though she probably hated him.

Some days he hated himself. Blamed himself for the pain he'd caused both him and Grace by letting her believe in him—even if it was for one short week. Had he told Grace right from the beginning that his son was not only dead, but Danny himself was responsible for Cory's accident, Grace would have happily kept her distance. She wouldn't have mourned the loss of his love, as he'd pictured her doing. He wouldn't have again felt the sting of living alone in his big, hollow house, torturously reminded of how it felt to be whole, to be wanted, to have people in his life and a purpose beyond perpetuating the family business.

But if nothing else had come from the week he'd spent with Grace and Sarah, Danny knew Grace would be fair. He thoroughly loved his daughter. He wanted to be part of her life, not just to assure she'd be ready to make a choice about Carson Services, but because he loved having her around. He loved being with her. And she was Danny's last chance at a family. He might never have the good fortune to share his life with Sarah's mother, but he could at least have a daughter.

So he supposed he'd come to this hearing as a show of good faith, proof that if Grace intended to let him have visitation, he wanted it. He suspected that any visitation she granted him would be supervised. He'd been the one in charge when Cory was killed. Grace's lawyer would undoubtedly drop that fact into the proceeding as a way to demonstrate that Danny wasn't a good dad. But he'd take even supervised visitation. At this point, he'd take anything he could get.

Grace entered the hearing room. Wearing an electric-blue suit, with her dark shoulder-length hair swaying around her and her sexy violet eyes shining, she was pretty enough to stop his heart. Yet in spite of how gorgeous she was, Danny's real reaction to her was emotional rather than physical. He'd missed her. They'd spent a total of nine days together. Three at his beach house and six at her house and he missed her. Ached for her. Longed for everything he knew darned well they could have had together, if he hadn't looked away for one split second and changed his destiny.

Grace approached the table with her lawyer, young, handsome, Robby Malloy. The guy Danny's lawyer called pretty boy Malloy. Danny could see why. He had the face of a movie star and carried himself like a billionaire. Danny experienced a surge of jealousy so intense he had to fight to keep himself from jumping from behind the table and yanking Grace away from the sleazy ambulance chaser.

But he didn't jump and he didn't yank. Because as a father his first concern had to be assuring that he was part of his daughter's life. He'd never had the right to care about Grace, about who she dated, or even if she dated.

So why was his blood pressure rising and his chest tightening from just looking at her with another man? Her lawyer no less? A man who may not even be romantically interested, only earning his hourly fee for representing her?

The judge entered the room, his dark robe billowing around him with his every step. Danny followed the lead of his attorney, Art Brown, and rose.

Having not yet taken his seat, Malloy extended his hand to the judge. "Judge Antanazzo."

"Good morning, Mr. Malloy," Charlie Antanazzo boomed. "How's my favorite attorney today?"

Malloy laughed. "Well, I doubt that I'm your favorite attorney," he said, obviously charming the judge. "But I'm great, your honor. This is my client, Grace McCartney."

As Grace shook Judge Antanazzo's hand, he smiled. "It's a pleasure to meet you."

Danny would just bet it was. Not only did the judge smile like any man happy to meet a pretty girl, but also Danny hadn't missed the way the judge took a quick inventory that started with Grace's shiny sable hair and managed to skim her perfect figure and nice legs in under a second.

This time it was a bit harder to refrain from leaping over the desk and yanking her to him.

But that ship had sailed and Danny had to grow accustomed to watching men fawn over Grace. He'd had his chance and he'd blown it. Or maybe it wasn't so much that Danny had had his chance, as much as it was that Danny had destroyed his own life long before he met Grace.

Danny's lawyer finally spoke. "Good morning, your honor," Art said, then shook the judge's hand. "This is my client, Danny Carson."

The judge quickly shook the hand Danny extended and frowned as he looked down at the brown case file he'd brought into the hearing room with him.

"Yes, I know. Danny Carson. CEO of Carson

Services. Let's see," he said, skimming the words in front of him. "Ms. McCartney was in your employ at one time." He continued reading. "She told you she was pregnant. You didn't believe her. Circumstances, including her being sick during the pregnancy, kept her from pursuing the matter. Then she took the baby to you." He read some more. "There's no record of child support." He looked at Danny. "Do you pay child support?"

Danny's lawyer said, "No, your honor, but—"

The judge ignored him. "All right then. This case boils down to a few concise facts. Ms. McCartney told you she was pregnant, brought the child to you and you don't pay child support." He glanced from Danny to Grace and held Grace's gaze. "Am I up to speed?

"There's a little more, your honor," Grace's lawyer said. "Once the court reporter is ready, I'd like to go on the record."

Danny's heart sank. Great. Just great. From the scant information the judge had read, it was pretty clear whose side he was on. Once Danny's past came out, the judge might not even let him have supervised visitation. The urge to defend himself rose up in Danny and this time rather than fight it, he let it take root. All the facts that the judge had read had made him look bad. But he wasn't. Everything he'd done wrong wasn't really a deliberate misdeed. Every one of his "bad" things were explainable—defendable.

He'd *misinterpreted* Grace's not answering the phone the night he'd flown home after his week of client hopping. As a result of that he broke off with her. So, when she came in to tell him she was pregnant, he'd thought it was a ruse to get him back, and he hadn't believed her. And when she left his employ, Danny had thought it was because her scheme had been exposed. He wasn't bad. He wasn't a schmuck. He had made some mistakes. Very defendable mistakes. Technically he could even defend himself about Cory's death.

He took a breath. That wasn't at issue right now. Sarah's custody was.

The lawyers and judge made preliminary statements for the record. Danny studiously avoided looking at Grace by tapping the eraser of his pencil on the desk. Eventually the judge said, "Mr. Malloy, ball's in your court."

"Thank you, your honor. My client would like to testify first."

Danny's lawyer had warned him that preliminary hearings could sometimes seem unofficial, but Danny shouldn't take it lightly because a court reporter would be recording the proceedings. He sat up a little straighter.

Though Grace stayed in her seat at the table, she was sworn in.

Her lawyer said, "Okay, Ms. McCartney, there is no argument between you and Mr. Carson about paternity?"

"No. And if there were we'd get a DNA test. We've agreed to that."

"But there's no need because you know Mr. Carson is the father?"

"Yes. I didn't—hadn't—" She paused, stumbling

over her explanation and Danny frowned, not sure what she was getting at.

"You hadn't had relations," Robbie prompted and Grace nodded.

"—I hadn't had relations with anybody for several months before Danny—Mr. Carson—and I spent a weekend at his beach house."

Danny damned near groaned. Not because it sounded as if he'd taken her to his private hideaway to seduce her, but because for the first time since that weekend he realized how important sleeping with him must have been in her life. She didn't sleep around. Hell, she apparently barely slept with anybody. But she'd been with him that night. She'd smiled at him, made him laugh, made him feel really alive—

Robbie Malloy said, "So why are you here today, Ms. McCartney?" bringing Danny back to the present.

"I'm here today because Mr. Carson and I had a shared custody agreement."

"Briefly, what does the agreement say?"

"That if he could stay at my house for two weeks, basically to learn how to care for Sarah, I would agree to shared custody."

"Did Mr. Carson want shared custody?"

"No. At first he wanted full custody. The agreement we made about shared custody was drafted to prevent us from fighting over Sarah. Shared custody seemed like the fair way to handle things."

"But—"

Grace took a breath. Danny raised his gaze to hers

and she looked directly at him. Which was exactly what he'd intended to make her do. If she wanted to testify against him, then let her do it looking into his eyes.

"But he didn't stay the two weeks."

Danny's eyes hardened.

"Ms. McCartney, is it also correct that he didn't sign the agreement?"

"No, he did not."

"And is that why we're here?"

"Well, I can't speak for Mr. Carson, but the reason I am here is to get it on the record that even though he didn't sign the agreement, or stay the two weeks, I believe Mr. Carson fulfilled its spirit and intent and I feel we should honor it."

"Which means you believe you and Mr. Carson should have shared custody?"

She held Danny's gaze. "Yes."

"You want me to have Sarah every other week?" Danny said, forgetting they were on the record.

"Yes. Danny, you proved yourself."

"I left."

"I know." She smiled slightly. "It doesn't matter. You showed me you can care for Sarah."

Robbie said, "Your honor, that's what we wanted to get on the record. No further questions."

The judge turned to Art. "Do you want to question Ms. McCartney?"

Art raised his hands. "Actually I think we'll let Ms. McCartney's testimony stand as is."

"Does Mr. Carson want to testify?"

Without consulting Danny, Art said, "No."

The judge quickly glanced down at his notes. "Technically you have a custody agreement in place. It's simply not executed. But Ms. McCartney still wants to honor it." He looked at Danny. "Mr. Carson? Do you want to honor the agreement?"

Danny nodded as Art said, "Yes."

The judge made a sound of strained patience, then said, "You're a very lucky man, Mr. Carson. Very lucky indeed."

Staring at Grace, who had begun casually gathering her purse as if what she had just said hadn't been of monumental significance, Danny didn't know what to say. Art spoke for him. "Your honor, when parents share custody it's frequently considered that each is taking his or her share of the financial burden when the child is with him—or her."

The judge closed the file. "Right. As if these two people have equal financial means." He faced Danny. "Don't screw this up." He left the room in a flurry or robes and promises about writing up an order.

Art began gathering his files. "Well, that went much better than expected," he said with a laugh, but over-whelmed with too many emotions to name, Danny watched Grace and her lawyer heading for the door.

Just as Grace would have stepped over the threshold, emotion overruled common sense and he called, "Wait!"

Grace turned and smiled at him.

Danny's throat worked. She was incredibly beauti-ful and incredibly generous. And he was numb with gratitude. "Why didn't you—"

She tilted her head in question. "Why didn't I what?"

Go for the jugular? Fight? Tell the court about Cory?

"Why are you letting me have Sarah?"

"You're her dad."

"I —" He took a breath. "What if I can't handle her?"

To his amazement, Grace laughed. "You can handle her. I've seen you handle her. You'll be fine."

"I'll be fine," he repeated, annoyed with Grace for being so flip, when the safety of their daughter was at stake. "What kind of answer is that!"

"It's an honest one."

"How can you trust her with me!"

"Are you telling me you're going to put her in danger?"

He glared at her. "You know I won't."

"Then there's no reason you shouldn't have your daughter."

"You trust me?"

She smiled. "I trust you. But if you're nervous, hire a nanny. You've told me at least twice that you were going to do that. So hire somebody."

Danny's heart swelled with joy. He was getting a second chance. He would have something of a family. He swallowed hard. "Okay."

She took two steps closer to him and placed her hand on his forearm. "Or, if you don't want to hire a nanny, you could come home."

Home. Her house *was* home. Warm. Welcoming. He could remember nearly every detail of their six short days. Especially how tempted he was to take what they both wanted. Just as he was tempted now to take what she was offering. A complete second chance. Not just an opportunity to be Sarah's daddy, but a second chance at life. A real life.

But he also knew he was damaged. So damaged it wasn't fair to use Grace as a step up out of his particular hell. He smiled regretfully. "You know you deserve better."

"So you say, but I don't think so. I see the part of you that you're trying to hide, or forget, or punish. I don't see the past."

"You're lucky."

"No, Danny, I'm not lucky. It's time. Time for you to move on." She held out her hand. "Come home with me. Start again."

He stared at the hand she offered. Delicate fingers. Pretty pink fingernails. Feminine things. Soft things. Things that had been missing from his life for so long. A million possibilities entered his head. A million things he would do, *could* do, if he took that hand, took the steps that would put him in Grace's world again. He could teach Sarah to walk. Hear her first word. Hear the first time she called him daddy. Sleep with Grace. Use the spaezle maker. Steal kisses. Share dreams. Spend Christmas as part of a family.

None of which he deserved.

"I can't."

CHAPTER TWELVE

DANNY turned away and though Grace's gut reaction was to demand that he talk to her, she didn't. Tears filled her eyes. Tears for him as much as for the wonderful future he was denying both of them, and she turned around and walked out of the hearing room.

Robbie was waiting. "You okay?"

She managed a smile. "Yeah. I'm fine."

"You're awfully generous with him."

"That's because he's so hard on himself."

"Be careful, Grace," Robbie said, directing her to the stairway that led to the courthouse lobby. "Men like Danny Carson who have a reputation for taking what they want don't like to lose. You may think that by "granting" him shared custody you were doing him and your daughter a kindness, but you had him over a barrel and he knew it. He may have just played you like a Stradivarius. Made you feel sorry for him so that you'd give him what he wanted, since he knew he probably couldn't beat you in court."

"I don't think so. I know Danny better than you do. He wouldn't do something like that."

"You think you know Danny?"

"I *know* Danny."

"Well, you better hope so because what we got on the record today—you saying you believed he was capable of caring for Sarah—negated any possibility we had of using his son's death in future hearings."

Grace gasped. "I would never use his son's death!"

Robbie held up his hand in defense. "Hey, I'm okay with that. Actually I agree that it would be cruel to use his son's death against him. I'm just saying be careful. This whole thing could backfire and you could end up fighting for your own daughter."

"I won't."

Robbie shook his head. "God save me from clients in love."

"It's that obvious?"

"Yes." Holding open one of the two huge double doors of the courthouse entrance, Robbie added, "And if Danny's as smart as everyone claims he is, he'll use it. Better put my number on speed dial."

Reading to Sarah in the rocking chair that night, Grace thought about the look on Danny's face when she stated for the record that she wanted their shared custody agreement upheld.

She shouldn't have been surprised that he expected her to testify against him. He was angry with himself and nothing she said or did could change that. No matter how sad he appeared or how much she'd simply wanted to hug him, she couldn't. A man who couldn't forgive himself, especially for something so traumatic, wasn't ready for a relationship and he might never be. It had broken her heart when he refused her offer to return home. As much for him as for herself.

But at least she had her answer now.

With Sarah asleep in her arms, Grace set the story-book on a shelf of the changing table and rose from the rocker. She laid Sarah in her crib, covered her, kissed her forehead and walked down the steps.

It wasn't going to be easy sharing custody with a man she loved but who could never love her. But she intended to do it. Actually she intended to do the one thing she'd promised herself she wouldn't do the night she rushed down to his beach house bar to see if he felt about her the way she felt about him. She was going to pine for him. She intended to love him forever, quietly, without expectation of anything in return because the real bottom line to Danny's trouble was that nobody had ever really loved him. At least not without expectation of anything in return. His parents expected him to take over the family business. His ex-wife held him responsible for their child's death. The people who worked for him wanted a job. His investors, even investors he considered friends, like Orlando, needed his expertise. Nobody loved him without expectation of anything in return.

So she would be that person. She might never be his wife, but she would be there for him in all the right ways, so that he could see that he was okay and that life didn't always have to be about what he could give somebody.

Two Mondays later when Robbie called and told her that the judge's order had come down, Grace sat quietly and listened as her lawyer explained how she was to have Sarah ready at six o'clock that Friday night. With every word he said, her chest tightened. Her eyes filled with tears. It was easy to say she intended to love Danny without expectation of anything in return when the situation was abstract. But now that shared custody was a reality she suddenly realized loving Danny meant denying herself. At the very least, she would spend every other week without her daughter.

She hung up the phone, glad for four days to prepare herself to see him, and managed to greet him with a smile Friday evening. With Sarah's diaper bag packed and sitting by the door, she put Sarah into his arms.

"Hey, Sarah Bear," he said softly and the baby hit him on the cheek with her rattle. He laughed nervously. "I guess she's forgotten who I am."

"Maybe," Grace said, trying to sound strong and confident, but with Danny standing at her door, refusing to go beyond the foyer, wearing a topcoat and scarf because western Pennsylvania had had its first snowfall of the season, it seemed as if the Danny she loved no longer existed. The guy in jeans and a T-shirt who made pancakes seemed to have been replaced by the man who ran Carson Services.

"We won't need that," Danny said, nodding at the diaper bag, as he struggled to contain Sarah who had begun to wail in earnest and stretched away from Danny, reaching for Grace. "I have a nursery full of things." For the first time since he'd arrived, he met her gaze. "I also hired a nanny."

"Good." Tears clogged Grace's throat when Sarah squealed and reached for her. "Stay with Daddy, Sarah," she whispered, pushing the baby back in Danny's arms, then fussing with Sarah's jacket as she slowly pulled her hands way.

But with her mom this close, Sarah all but crawled out of Danny's arms again, with a squeal that renewed her crying.

Pain ricocheted through Grace. "Maybe we should have broken this up? Had her do an overnight visit or two before we forced her to spend an entire week."

"It's going to be hard no matter how we do it. Let's just get this over with."

He opened the door, not even sparing Grace a glance, taking her daughter.

"If she gives you any trouble, just call," Grace said, trying to keep her voice light and bright as he walked away, but it wobbled.

Already on the sidewalk, striding to his car, Danny said, "We're fine."

And he left.

Watching his car lights as they disappeared into the night, Grace stood on her stoop, with her lawyer's words ringing in her ears, suddenly wondering if Danny really hadn't tricked her.

Could he have put on jeans a few times, made a couple of pancakes and cruelly lured her into loving him, all to take her child?

* * *

Danny entered his home, sobbing Sarah on his arm. "Elise!" he called, summoning his nanny.

She strode into the foyer. Tall and sturdily build, Elise wore a brightly colored knit cardigan over a white blouse and gray skirt. She looked like she could have stepped out of a storybook, as the quintessential nanny.

"Oh, my. This little one's got a pair of lungs!" Elise said with a laugh, and reached out to take Sarah from his arms. But as Danny handed the baby to her nanny, he felt odd about giving over Sarah's care so easily. He remembered that Grace had told him that she didn't want to share his nanny because caring for Sarah was part of her quality time.

After shrugging out of his topcoat, he reached for Sarah again. "Tonight, I'll take care of her."

"But—"

"At least until she adjusts to being here."

Elise took a breath, gave him a confused smile and said, "As you wish."

Danny didn't care what she thought. All he cared about was Sarah. He'd thought hiring a nanny would be the perfect way to help ease Sarah into her new life, but seeing Elise with Sarah felt wrong. Sarah was his responsibility. His little girl. His daughter.

Carrying Sarah into the nursery, Danny thought of Grace. How tears had filled her eyes when Sarah had begun to cry. He'd left quickly, not to cause her pain, but to get all three of them accustomed to this every other Friday night ritual. But he'd hurt her.

Again.

It seemed he was always hurting Grace.

Still, with crying Sarah on his arm, it wasn't the time to think about that. He wrestled her out of her jacket, little black shoes, tiny jeans and T-shirt, then rolled her into a pair of pajamas.

She never stopped crying.

He put her on his shoulder and patted her back, as he walked downstairs and to the refrigerator where he extracted one of the bottles Elise had prepared. Sitting on the rocker in the nursery, he fed her the bottle and though she drank greedily, sniffled remnants of her crying jag accompanied her sucking. The second the bottle came out of her mouth, she began to cry again.

"I'm sorry. I know this is hard. I know you miss your mom, but this is the right thing. Trust me."

He paced the floor with her, trying to comfort her, but as he pivoted to make his third swipe across the room, he saw the books beside the rocker. The designer he'd hired to create the yellow and pink, bear-theme room had strategically stationed books on a low table within reach of the rocker. After sitting again, he took one of the books, opened it and began to read.

"Once upon a time, in a kingdom far away, there lived a princess. Her name was—" He paused, then smiled. "Sarah. Sarah bear."

Sarah's crying slowed.

"She was a beautiful child with blond—reddish-brown curls," he amended, matching the description of the little girl in the book to the little girl in his arms. "And blue eyes."

Her crying reduced to sniffles and she blinked, her confused expression taking him back to the first night he'd cared for her alone—the night Grace had been edgy. The memory caused him to smile. He hadn't wanted to be alone with Sarah. Wasn't sure he could handle her. He'd only kept the baby to please Grace.

He took a breath. This time he was caring for Sarah to *protect* Grace. From him. Adding a failed marriage to ignoring her pregnancy and taking her child wouldn't help anything. He had to remember that.

"The princess lived alone with her father, the king. Her mother had died when the princess was a baby and a governess had been hired. Mrs. Pickleberry had a face puckered in a perpetual frown and Sarah would pretend to be ill, rather than spend time with her when the king was out of the palace performing his royal duties. Each time, when Mrs. Pickleberry would leave her room, sufficiently convinced that Sarah should stay in bed for the day, Sarah would crawl into her window seat, her legs tucked beneath her, her thumb in her mouth, watching, alone, for her father to return."

Danny stopped reading. The king didn't have a choice about leaving his daughter in the care of her governess, but Danny had choices. Lots of them. In the argument they'd had the day Grace brought Sarah to him, Grace had asked if it was better for Sarah to be raised by strangers rather than her mother. Still, that wasn't what was happening here. Yes, Sarah would be stuck with a governess—uh, nanny—while Danny was at work, but he wasn't taking Sarah away from her mother. Not really. Just every other week.

He glanced down. Sarah was asleep.

Thank God. He didn't think he could take any more of the story's inadvertent accusations. He laid the baby in her crib and stood for several minutes, just watching Sarah, basking in the joy of being a dad, considering all the things he could do for Sarah, and convincing himself that while he had Sarah, Grace could also do so many things, things she otherwise didn't have time to do.

But the soft smile that had lit his face suddenly died. Grace might have time to do tons of different things, but she wouldn't. She would spend every hour he had custody worrying about Sarah. Not because Danny wasn't trustworthy, but because she would miss her. And only because she would miss her. In fact, right now, Grace was probably crying, or lonely. And he absolutely couldn't stand the thought of it.

He wasn't the kind of man to hurt people. But his reasoning this time went beyond his own image of himself. He couldn't stand the thought of Grace missing Sarah because he loved her. The last thing any man wanted to do was hurt the woman he loved most in this world. And yet that was what he always did with Grace. He hurt her. When he'd met her, he was a broken, empty man. She'd reminded him of life. That Sunday night at the beach house, she'd given him a glimpse of what they'd have together if he could open up. When he couldn't, she'd gracefully accepted that he didn't want to see her anymore. But when she'd gotten pregnant, she'd tried one more time. When he rejected her again, she didn't return until she had Sarah. Offering him something he truly didn't deserve: a place in their daughter's life. A place she hadn't snatched away. Even knowing his dark secret, she had faith in him when he had none in himself.

Danny gritted his teeth. He knew the solution to this problem. He knew it as well as he knew his own last name.

In order to save Grace, he had to let go of his guilt. He had to try again. In earnest.

Or he had to take Sarah back to Grace. For good. No more shared custody.

Halfway to the kitchen to make cocoa, Grace heard a knock on her door and peered at her watch. Who would be visiting after nine at night?

Expecting it to be her parents, who were undoubtedly worried about her because this was her first night without Sarah, she turned and headed for the door. When she looked through the peephole and saw Danny holding sleeping Sarah, she jumped back and yanked open the door.

Reaching for Sarah, she said, "What happened? What's wrong?"

He motioned inside her house. "Can we talk?"

Cradling Sarah on her arm, she looked down and

examined every exposed inch of her sleeping baby. Her gaze shooting to Danny, she said, "She's fine?"

He nodded. "Yeah. It's you and I who have the problem. We need to talk."

Grace's heart stopped. She'd nearly had herself convinced that Robbie was right. Danny had tricked her and he had gotten everything he wanted at Grace's expense. All because she'd fallen in love with him.

But he was back, saying they needed to talk, sounding like a man ready to give, rather than take. Still, this time she had to be strong, careful. She couldn't fall victim to the look in his beautiful dark eyes...or the hope in her heart.

She had to be strong.

"Danny, it's late and our lawyers said everything we needed to say—"

"Not mine. He hardly said anything. And there are a few things I need to say. Put Sarah to bed. In *her* bed."

The gentleness of his voice got to her. If nothing else, Grace knew with absolute certainty that Danny loved Sarah. Knowing her lawyer would probably be angry that she talked to Danny without counsel, Grace stepped aside so Danny could enter.

As she turned to walk up the steps with the baby, she saw Danny hesitate in her small entryway.

Remembering he was always more at ease in her home when she gave him something to do, she said, "I was just about to make cocoa. You could go in the kitchen and get mugs."

"Okay."

When she returned downstairs, Grace saw he had only gotten as far as the stools in front of the breakfast counter. Again noting his hesitation, Grace said, "Don't you want cocoa?"

"I'd love some."

He sounded so quiet and so unsteady that Grace didn't know what to say. She set the pan on the stove and poured in milk and cocoa, waiting for him to talk. When he didn't, she lowered the flame on the gas burner and walked to the breakfast bar.

"Did something happen with Sarah?"

"No. She was fine." He caught her gaze. "Why did you do this? Why are you letting me have her every other week?"

She shrugged. "You're Sarah's dad. She loves you. You love her."

He caught her gaze. "And that's it?"

"What else is there?"

"You didn't give Sarah to me to try to force my hand?"

"Force your hand?" She laughed. "Oh, my God, Danny, when have I ever gotten you to do anything? You didn't believe I slept with you because I liked you. You were sure I had an agenda. You didn't believe I was pregnant when I told you. You kicked me out of your office. You were so suspicious of me when I suggested shared custody that *you* insisted on the agreement. If there's one thing I know not to do it's try to force you to do anything."

"You didn't give me Sarah so that I'd be so grateful I'd fall in love with you?"

After a second to recover from the shock of that accusation, she shook her head sadly. He really did believe that people only did nice things when they wanted something from him. "Oh, Danny, I didn't give you time with Sarah to drag you into a relationship with me."

"Really?"

"Yes. I gave you time with Sarah because you're her dad."

"And you want nothing from me."

Grace debated lying to him. She *wanted* them to be a normal family. She wanted him to be the happy, laughing guy who'd made love to her at the beach house. She wanted him to want her. To welcome her into his life with open arms. She wanted a lot, but she didn't expect anything from him. The way she saw their lives unfolding, she would spend most of the time they had together just happy to see him unwind.

But if there was one thing she'd learned about Danny over the past weeks, it was that he valued honesty. So she took a breath and said, "I want a lot. But I'm also a realist. You won't fall in love again until you're ready. Nobody's going to push you."

He slid onto the stool. "I know." Pointing at the stove, he said, "I think your pot's boiling over."

"Eeek!" She spun away from the breakfast bar and ran to the stove, where hot milk bubbled over the sides of her aluminum pot. "Looks like I'll be starting over."

"I think we should both start over."

Not at all sure what he meant by that, Grace poured

out the burned milk and filled the dirty pot with water, her heart pounding at the possibilities. "And how do you propose we start over?"

"The first step is that I have to tell you everything."

She found a second pot, filled it with milk and poured in cocoa, again refusing to hurry him along or push him. This was his show. She would let him do whatever he wanted. She'd *never* misinterpret him again. "So tell me everything."

While she adjusted the gas burner, he said, "Tonight I really thought through the things that had had happened to me in the past several years, and I realized something I'd refused to see before this."

He paused again. Recognizing he might think she wasn't paying attention, Grace said, "And what was that?"

"My marriage to Lydia was over before Cory's accident."

At that Grace turned to face him. "What?"

"Tonight when I was caring for Sarah in my brand-new nursery and thinking about how sad you probably were here alone, I realized that you are very different from Lydia. She and I spent most of our married life fighting. First she didn't want children, then when we had Cory she wanted him enrolled in a school for gifted children in California. We didn't fight over my pushing him into taking over Carson Services. We fought because she kept pushing him away. She didn't want him around."

"Oh."

"I won't say I didn't love her when I married her, but I can now see that we were so different, especially in what we wanted out of life, that we were heading for divorce long before Cory's accident. Tonight, I finally saw that I needed to separate the two. Cory's accident didn't ruin my marriage. Lydia and I had handled that all by ourselves."

"I'm sorry."

He laughed lightly. "You know what? I knew you would be. And I think that's part of why I like you. Why I was drawn to you at the beach house. You really have a sixth sense about people. I saw how you were with Orlando and listened in sometimes on your conversations, and I knew you were somebody special. More than that, though, you respected the same things I did. Especially family and commitments. You and I had the thing Lydia and I lacked. Common beliefs. Sunday night when we were alone, I realized we also had more than our fair share of chemistry." He paused, then said, "But I panicked."

Since Grace couldn't dispute what he said—or add to it—she stayed silent, letting him talk.

"Tonight, rocking Sarah, thinking about you, hating that you had to give up your child, I was angry that life had forced us into this position, but I suddenly realized it wasn't life that forced us here. It was me because I didn't think I could love you without hurting you."

Too afraid to make a hopeful guess about the end of his conclusions, Grace held her breath.

"I guess thinking about my own marriage and Lydia

and Cory while holding Sarah, I finally saw something that made everything fall into place for me."

Grace whispered, "What's that?"

"That if you and I had been married, we would have weathered Cory's death. You might have honestly acknowledged my mistake in grabbing my cell phone, and even acknowledged that I would feel guilty, but you never would have let me take the blame. You and I would have survived. A marriage between us would have survived."

Grace pressed her hand to her chest. "That's quite a compliment."

"You're a very special person. Or maybe the strength of your love is special." He shook his head. "Or maybe you and I together are special. I don't know. I just know that through all this you'd been very patient. But I'm done running."

She smiled. "Thought you didn't run."

"Well, maybe I wasn't running. Maybe I was holding everybody back. Away. But I can't do that anymore."

She took a breath, her hope building, her heart pounding.

"Because I love you. I love you." He repeated, as if saying it seemed so amazing he needed to say it again. "I couldn't stand the thought of you here alone, and though I don't want to hurt you I finally saw that unless I took this step, I would always be hurting you."

Her voice a mere whisper, Grace said, "What step?"

"I want to love you. I want you to marry me."

She would have been content to hear him say he

wanted to try dating. His proposal was so far beyond what she'd been expecting that her breath stuttered in her chest. "What?"

"I love you and I want you to marry me."

Dumbstruck, Grace only stared at him.

"You could say you love me, too."

"I love you, too."

At that Danny laughed. The sound filled the small kitchen.

"And you want to marry me." He took a breath. "Grace, alone with Sarah I realized I had everything I needed and I could have talked myself into accepting only that. But I want you, too. Will you marry me?"

"And I want to marry you!" She made a move to launch herself into his arms, but remembered her cocoa and turned to flip off the burner. By the time she turned back, he was at her side, arms opened, ready for her to walk into them.

He wrapped his arms around her as his mouth met hers. Without a second of hesitation, Grace returned his kiss, opening her mouth when he nudged her to do so. Her heart pounded in her ears as her pulse began to scramble. He loved her. *He loved her and wanted to marry her.* It almost seemed too good to be true.

He pulled away. "Pot's probably boiling over."

"I thought I turned that off." She whirled away from him and saw the cooling pot. "I did turn that off."

"I have a better idea than cocoa anyway."

He pulled her to him and whispered something in her ear that should have made a new mother blush. But she laughed and countered something equally sexy in his ear and he kissed her deeply, reminding her of her thoughts driving up I-64 the Monday they left Virginia Beach. *She'd found Mr. Right.*

She *had* found Mr. Right, and they were about to live happily ever after.

EPILOGUE

RESTING UNDER the shade of a huge oak, on the bench seat of a weathered wooden picnic table, Grace watched Sarah as she played in the sandbox with the children of Grace's cousins. She could also see Danny standing in left field, participating in the married against the singles softball game at the annual McCartney reunion.

The CEO and chairman of the board of Carson Services didn't look out of place in his khaki shorts and T-shirt, as Grace expected he might. It wasn't even odd to see him punching his fist into the worn leather baseball mitt he found in his attic. Everything about this day seemed perfectly normal.

The batter hunkered down, preparing for a pitch thrown so hard Grace barely saw the ball as it sliced through the air toward the batter's box, but her cousin Mark had seen it. His bat connected at just the right time to send the ball sailing through the air, directly at Danny.

With a groan, she slapped her hands over her eyes, but unable to resist, spread her fingers and peeked through. The ball sped toward Danny like a comet.

He yelled, "No worries. I've got it." Punching his fist into his mitt twice before he held it up and the ball smacked into place with a crack.

Whoops of joy erupted from the married team because Danny had made the final out of the game. For the first time in almost twenty years, the married men had beaten the younger, more energetic singles.

Danny received a round of congratulations and praise. He was new blood. Exactly what the family needed. Grace sat a bit taller on the bench seat, glancing at eighteen-month-old Sarah, who happily shoveled sand into the empty bed of a plastic dump truck.

The married team disbursed to brag to their wives about the softball victory. The singles grumbled that Danny was a ringer. Danny jogged over to Grace looking like a man about to receive Olympic gold.

"Did you see that?"

"Yes. You were great."

"I was, wasn't I?"

Grace laughed. "Men." She took a quiet breath and he sat down on the bench seat beside her.

"Are you okay?"

"I'm fine."

"You're sure?"

"I'm sure."

"It's just that the last time you were pregnant you were sick—"

She put her hand over his mouth to shut him up. "For the one-hundred-and-twenty-seven-thousand-two-hundred-and-eighty-fourth time, all pregnancies are different. Yes, I was sick with Sarah. But I'm only a little bit queasy this time."

She pulled her hand away and he said, "Maybe you were sick because—"

She put her hand over his mouth again. "I was not sick because I went through that pregnancy alone. We've been over this, Danny." Because he was so funny, she laughed. "A million times."

"Or at least one-hundred-and-twenty-seven-thou-sand-two-hundred-and-eighty-four."

She laughed again and he glanced around the property. "This is a beautiful place."

"That's why we have the picnic here every year. There are no distractions. Just open space, trees for shade and a brick grill to make burgers and keep our side dishes warm. So everybody has time to talk, to catch up with what the family's been doing all year."

"It's great."

"It is great."

"And your family's very nice."

She smiled. "They like you, too."

He took a satisfied breath. "Do you want me to watch Sarah for a while?"

"No. It's okay. You keep mingling. We're fine."

"But this is your family."

"And I'm mingling. Women mingle more around the food and the sandbox. At one point or another I'll see everybody." She grinned. "Besides, this may be your last day out with people for a while. You should take advantage of it."

"What are you talking about? I have to go to work tomorrow."

"Right." She rolled her eyes with a chuckle. "Tomorrow you're going to be suffering. Every muscle in your body will be screaming. You'll need a hot shower just to be able to put on your suit jacket."

He straightened on the bench seat. "Hey, I will not be sore."

"Yes, you will."

"I am an athlete."

"You push papers for a living and work out at the gym a few nights a week." She caught his gaze, then pressed a quick kiss to his lips. "You are going to be in bed for days."

The idea seemed to please him because he grinned. "Will you stay in bed with me?"

"And let Sarah alone to fend for herself with Pickleberry?" They'd found Elise to be such a stickler for rules that Danny and Grace had nicknamed her after the governess in the storybook.

"Hey, you're the one who said to keep her."

"Only so we wouldn't be tempted to overuse her."

At that Danny laughed. He laughed long and hard and Grace smiled as she studied him. All traces of his guilt were gone. He remembered his son fondly now. He'd even visited the next-door neighbor who had been driving the SUV and they'd come to terms with the tragedy enough that Mrs. Oliver was a regular visitor at their home.

He'd also hired a new vice president and delegated

at least half of his responsibility to him, so they could spend the majority of their summer at the beach house in Virginia Beach. He loved Sarah. He wanted a big family and Grace was happy to oblige. Not to give him heirs, but because he loved her.

Completely. Honestly. And with a passion that hadn't died. Their intense love for each other seemed to grow every day. He had a home and she had a man who would walk to the ends of the earth for her.

Watching her other family members as they mingled and laughed, weaving around the big oak trees, sharing cobbler recipes and tales about their children, Grace suddenly saw that was the way it was meant to be.

That was the lesson she'd learned growing up among people who didn't hesitate to love.

Somewhere out there, there was somebody for everybody.

* * * * *

HARLEQUIN® Romance.

New York Times bestselling author

DIANA PALMER

Handsome, eligible ranch owner Stuart York knew Ivy Conley was too young for him, so he closed his heart to her and sent her away—despite the fireworks between them. Now, years later, Ivy is determined not to be treated like a little girl anymore…but for some reason, Stuart is always fighting her battles for her. And safe in Stuart's arms makes Ivy feel like a woman…his woman.

Winter Roses

Available November.

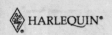

EVERLASTING LOVE™

Every great love has a story to tell™

Charlie fell in love with Rose Kaufman
before he even met her, through stories her
husband, Joe, used to tell. When Joe is killed
in the trenches, Charlie helps Rose through
her grief and they make a new life together.
But for Charlie, a question remains—can
love be as true the second time around?
Only one woman can answer that....

Look for

*The Soldier and
the Rose*

by
Linda Barrett

Available November wherever you buy books.

HARLEQUIN®

Mediterranean NIGHTS™

*Not everything is above board
on Alexandra's Dream!*

*Enjoy plenty of secrets, drama and sensuality
in the latest from Mediterranean Nights.*

Coming in November 2007...

BELOW DECK

by

Dorien Kelly

Determined to protect her young son,
widow Mei Lin Wang keeps him hidden
aboard *Alexandra's Dream* under cover of
her job. But life gets extremely complicated
when the ship's security officer, Gideon Dayan,
is piqued by the mystery surrounding this
beautiful, haunted woman....

REQUEST YOUR FREE BOOKS!
2 FREE NOVELS PLUS 2
FREE GIFTS!

HARLEQUIN ROMANCE®

From the Heart, For the Heart

YES! Please send me 2 FREE Harlequin Romance® novels and my 2 FREE gifts. After receiving them, if I don't wish to receive any more books, I can return the shipping statement marked "cancel." If I don't cancel, I will receive 4 brand-new novels every month and be billed just $3.57 per book in the U.S., or $4.05 per book in Canada, plus 25¢ shipping and handling per book and applicable taxes, if any*. That's a savings of over 15% off the cover price! I understand that accepting the 2 free books and gifts places me under no obligation to buy anything. I can always return a shipment and cancel at any time. Even if I never buy another book from Harlequin, the two free books and gifts are mine to keep forever.

114 HDN EEV7 314 HDN EEWK

Name	(PLEASE PRINT)	
Address		Apt.
City	State/Prov.	Zip/Postal Code

Signature (if under 18, a parent or guardian must sign)

Mail to the **Harlequin Reader Service®**:
IN U.S.A.: P.O. Box 1867, Buffalo, NY 14240-1867
IN CANADA: P.O. Box 609, Fort Erie, Ontario L2A 5X3

Not valid to current Harlequin Romance subscribers.

Want to try two free books from another line?
Call 1-800-873-8635 or visit www.morefreebooks.com.

* Terms and prices subject to change without notice. NY residents add applicable sales tax. Canadian residents will be charged applicable provincial taxes and GST. This offer is limited to one order per household. All orders subject to approval. Credit or debit balances in a customer's account(s) may be offset by any other outstanding balance owed by or to the customer. Please allow 4 to 6 weeks for delivery.

Your Privacy: Harlequin is committed to protecting your privacy. Our Privacy Policy is available online at www.eHarlequin.com or upon request from the Reader Service. From time to time we make our lists of customers available to reputable firms who may have a product or service of interest to you. If you would prefer we not share your name and address, please check here. ☐

HR07

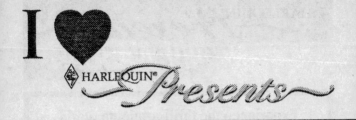

HARLEQUIN *Romance*

Coming Next Month

Fall in love with our ranchers, bosses and single dads in a month filled with mistletoe and magic, and where happy endings are guaranteed!

#3985 WINTER ROSES Diana Palmer
Long, Tall Texans
Rugged rancher Stuart has always been protective of innocent Ivy. Growing up and finding your place in the world is tough, but there's nowhere Ivy feels more like a woman than in Stuart's arms. A fantastic new book from an award-winning author.

#3986 THE COWBOY'S CHRISTMAS PROPOSAL Judy Christenberry
Mistletoe & Marriage
The first book in this festive duet that's sure to get you in the Christmas mood. Penny has just inherited her family ranch, but she has a problem... she doesn't know how to run it! Luckily, help is at hand in the form of Jake, the gorgeous cowboy next door....

#3987 APPOINTMENT AT THE ALTAR Jessica Hart
Bridegroom Boss
Free spirit Lucy doesn't like being told what to do, so when irresistible tycoon Guy challenges her to find a real job, she does—as Guy's assistant! Don't miss the second book in this wonderful duet.

#3988 THE BOSS'S DOUBLE TROUBLE TWINS Raye Morgan
9 to 5
Don't you just love surprises? Workaholic businessman Mitch gets a big one when new employee and old flame Darcy gives him news that will change his life—he's going to be a daddy, to twins!

#3989 CARING FOR HIS BABY Caroline Anderson
Heart to Heart
Everyone makes mistakes, and sometimes second chances can be even sweeter than the first time around. When Emily opens her door to Harry, the man who broke her heart years before, he is cradling a little baby in his arms. How can she resist?

#3990 MIRACLE ON CHRISTMAS EVE Shirley Jump
If you love this joyful season, don't miss single father C.J. struggling with newfound fatherhood, and yearning for a magical Christmas. Jessica's heart is quickly won by C.J.'s enchanting daughter, but what about the man himself?

HRCNM1007